THE YEAR OF
THE WOOD-DRAGON

BY

ACHMED ABDULLAH

AUTHOR OF "THE SWINGING CARAVAN," ETC.

ILLUSTRATED BY
FRANK DOBIAS

NEW YORK
BRENTANO'S
PUBLISHERS

PRINTED IN THE UNITED STATES OF AMERICA

THE VAIL-BALLOU PRESS
BINGHAMTON AND NEW YORK

CHAPTER I

HE was only ten years of age at the time; but he never forgot the scene. The picture of it, and his father's words which accompanied it, remained graven deeply in the back cells of his brain.

He was playing on the street outside with Mehmet Tugluk, the Afghan mutton-butcher's son, and Gandra Rai, the first-born of the low-caste Hindu sweeper. Their game was really "London Bridge is Falling Down," only they called it *"Iftahu el Bab*—Open the Gate." A wandering Moslem priest from Mecca had taught it to them. And, instead of proclaiming that the old bridge was "falling down, falling down, my fair lady," they chanted in a doleful, minor key: "Open the gate for me and my carriage to enter," and they laughed and yelled and quarreled and made up in spite of the brazen mid-day heat that had driven all the shopkeepers of the neighborhood to shelter and siesta behind closed shutters.

Overhead bloated the crimson, exaggerated sun of the tropics, sending down rays like crackling spears, drying the slimy puddles where the tiny, blue-snouted buffaloes loved to roll and grunt, and gilding the rickety, greasy wilderness of houses where he lived: the Kashmiri bazar quarter, the native slums of this little North-Indian town of Chawkpore that nestled in a fold of the Himalaya foothills.

The place was a melting-pot of half Asia's riotous, colorful breeds.   Only—contrary to the great American melting-pot—here, in India, the races did not happen to melt very much.   Many races were here besides North-India's varied, indigenous tribes: Persians, with their high, peaked, sombre caps of Astrakan fur; Arabs, in biblical costumes, stalking proudly, independently; Tamalis from the far south of India, gentle, mild-mannered, very dark, but with finely cut, highly-bred, intelligent features; a sprinkling of Malays and Burmese and Chinese ambling along on padded slippers.   There were here corpulent Buniah bankers from Kootch and Goojerat, with their fantastic pyramids of white muslin crowning bullet-shaped heads, raising their voices in rivalry with the raucous, coarse accents of swaggering Kabul and Scinde "roughnecks," ever ready to pick a quarrel and strike a blow.

The Tower of Babel could not have assembled at its foundation a more complete collection of the human race. Palanquins, native carriages surmounted by domes of red, gaily embroidered domes beneath which dusky beauties concealed themselves, passed by, drawn by beautiful, tiny, snow-white oxen from Surat, as well as motor-cars with British officers and civil servants, or Wealthy British or native merchants. The streets were bordered by small booths the flooring of which, raised several feet above the roadway, served 'for counter and stall. Everything was for sale here.

For this was an important enough trade centre, where the men of the plains swapped their produce and that of Liverpool and Hamburg and Chicago against the rough wares brought from across the frozen passes by the yellow-faced, duffel-clad Tibetan hillmen. To the northwest, sharply etched against the tight, pigeon-blue sky, towered the fantastic crags and peaks of the higher mountains.

Up there was the silvery glint of the eternal snows, and, ever since he had been a small baby, he had been conscious of a certain longing, a certain homesickness for the snows and the cool cleanliness of the snows.

It was perhaps a racial inheritance bequeathed to him by his father; an inheritance of which he hardly realized the meaning. For scarcely, if ever, did he think of the fact that, in spite of his sun-tanned skin, his ragged dress of a poor, native boy, his speech in which he handled Hindu and the Tibetan dialects of the foothills with greater fluency than English, his tolerance, call it superstition if you prefer, which caused him to give equal reverence to Moslem dervish, Brahmin priest and an occasional red-capped Lamaist abbot from the north, from Gyantse or mysterious Lhassa—that, in spite of all this, he was white and Christian. The Chawkpore slums had swallowed him, as they had swallowed his father who, a gifted young artist, had come to India years earlier to paint the blues and greens and pottery-reds of that strange land and who had remained, a poor white man living like a native, cut off from his own race through poverty and shame, keeping a small shop, sucked under by the whirlpool of turbaned humanity. He did not remember his mother. She had been an English girl, born in India, the daughter of some minor government official; had died in a cholera epidemic when he had been less than two years of age. So here he was on the street, playing the Indian equivalent for "London Bridge" with Mehmet Tugluk and Gandra Rai.

"What do you want?" he demanded laughing, according to the rules of the game, "the grapes or the figs?"

"Hayah! Hayah!" cut in the shrill cry of Mara, the lean, middle-aged, low-caste Hindu woman who was his father's housekeeper and business partner, as she rushed out of the house and up to him. "Quick!" she implored. "Come quick, little piece of my soul!"

"What is it, Mara?"

"Your father wants you!"

"All right. Just wait till we have finished the game."

"No, no. He wants you at once. Come. There is no time to be lost!"

She took the boy's hand, and they crossed the outer room, which was the shop, at a run. It was a miserable little cubicle of a place, with a wooden, unpainted counter, the stock-in-trade thrown in dusty confusion about the ground; a matting full of yellow Persian leaf tobacco and pipe bowls of scarlet clay, a palm leaf bag containing lumps of coarse, white-brown sugar, a little arsenic, cheap French scents and scaps, henna and rouge. From hooks on the walls were suspended reeds for pipes, tallow candles, cigarette papers, and dirty wax tapers, and to one side there was a *mastabah,* a low earthen platform, for the customers and a palm-wool stool for the master of the shop.   But the latter was now in the back room, stretched out on a string bed, taken by a sudden, deadly illness, his blue eyes already half glazed, his emaciated hands pulling nervously, helplessly, at his long, unkempt, grey-streaked beard, as if trying to hold back his ebbing life.

The Hindu woman commenced fanning his fevered face with a dry palm leaf.   But the man sent her from the room with a kindly word:

"Go, faithful old Mara!   I want to talk to my son!"

And then there came that scene which the boy never forgot.

His father raised himself on his elbows with his last remaining strength.   He turned to him, speaking with a great, driving seriousness.

"Jimmie," he said, "there are so many things I wanted to do, for you and for myself.   But I always waited until the next day; and—" very gently, apologetically—"there is going to be no more next day—not for me——"

"Father—please——"

"Hurts you to see me die, Jimmie?   Of course it does.   You are fond of me—and I am fond of you.   But I am going—no use denying it. And I haven't the time to tell you all the things about me and about yourself you ought to know. You'll have to make your own way—you see—" pointing through the sleazy curtains that divided

the front from the back room and whence came
the voices of a Hindu coolie haggling over an
ounce of henna—"the little shop belongs to Mara
much more than to me. She'll take care of you
as long as she can, as long as you are too young.
Afterwards—yes—you'll have to make your own
way, here, in India, in a strange land——"

"It isn't a strange land, father!" he replied.

"Isn't it?" The older man smiled—a lop-
sided, rather pathetic smile.

"Why—no! It's my own!"

"You are wrong, son!"

"Wrong? How?"

"Because you are Jimmie Weatherby. Remember that!" The older man was now utterly
serious; he stared into his son's eyes with all his
latent strength, with every ounce of energy that
remained in his sick body. "Remember that!"
he said again, his voice rising a little. "James
Clinton Weatherby! Repeat it, will you?"

"James—Clinton—Weatherby!" the boy echoed, rather wonderingly, his eyes filling with
hot tears.

"That's right!" smiled the father. "James
Clinton Weatherby! And don't you forget it.
Promise!"

"I promise, father!"

"And don't you forget either that you are an
American and a gentleman—as I am an American

and—" he slurred, stopped, continued—"as once I was a gentleman."

"What is a gentleman?" came the boy's naive question.

"Don't you know? Well—it's hard to explain, Jimmie. But I guess a gentleman is somebody who thinks right and does right—or, rather, who does right as he thinks it right. Do you understand?"

"Yes—" the boy puzzled—"I believe I do. For instance—" he interrupted himself, considered, and went on: "The other day, when Mehmet Tugluk tried to steal from the blind old beggar near the Mosque a bunch of bananas that somebody had given him—and when I prevented him—was I—oh—" with ingenuously self-conscious pride—"was I a gentleman?"

"Absolutely, son. But—there's another meaning, too, to the word. You see, when people have been gentlemen for generations—from father to son and so forth—then the quality—well —it sort of descends—don't you see—is inherited? You can tell by a fellow's very name—or at least ought to. So it is with your last two names: 'Clinton' and 'Weatherby.' Both families have always—well—nearly always—thought right and acted right. So the names are good names, proud names, back home in America—

just like—oh—for instance—some great Rajah's
name here in India. . . ."

"Like the Mahratta Rajahs who have always
fought bravely, father?"

"Exactly. Good comparison. You are getting what I mean, son. 'Clinton' and 'Weatherby'—good names—Rajahs' names back home!
And that's all I am leaving you, Jimmie: two
names and—" again he smiled—"a bit of advice.
Don't make the same mistake that I did. Don't
you ever wait for the next day. Think—think
well—then do—at once! Will you remember
that?"

"Yes, father!"

"All right. Repeat after me: Think—think
well—then do—at once!"

"Think—" the boy echoed—"think well—
then do—at once!"

"All right, Jimmie!"

So his father died. So his father was buried
by his native friends, the Afghan mutton-butcher,
the low-caste Hindu sweeper, the Tibetan hide
and salt merchant at the end of the Kashmiri
bazar, and the flat-faced, Nepalese coppersmith;
poor men who paid for the burial because of the
compassion and pity in their hearts, and because
the European residents of Chawkpore, if indeed
they knew, did not care. To them the yellow-

bearded, blue-eyed shopkeeper—and doubtless they were right according to the limits of their understanding—had been just another one of those white men gone to seed, swallowed by the brown maelstrom of Hindustan.

Jimmie did not forget what his father had told him, though at first the words were only words to him, with not much meaning or significance.

"I am James Clinton Weatherby!" he would say to himself, wonderingly, only half comprehending, as he played in the streets; in the evenings, when he came home and helped faithful old Mara with the cooking and the cleaning; at night, when he fell asleep on his cot while from the Jain temple, not far away, there drifted in the savage braying of the conches, the chanting of the worshippers before the shrines, the hollow thump of gongs and tomtoms, and at times an acrid aroma of incense smoke and marigold.

"I am James Clinton Weatherby!" he said one day, rather challengingly, to Abdesalam Tugluk, the Afghan mutton-butcher, when he had teased the latter beyond endurance and when the Afghan had threatened him with a heavy thorn stick.

"You are a son of the devil, clumsy and decidedly unbeautiful!" Abdesalam Tugluk replied. Then he laughed, and Jimmie joined in the laughter.

So he lived the haphazard life of Eastern child-hood, with no lessons but those of the crooked, crowded streets and bazars, and an occasional word of prosy wisdom, Moslem or Hindu or Buddhist, from some grey-beard among his fa-ther's former customers and friends.

These latter were men of many races and faiths and castes, of many trades. Some were sweepers—lowest of the low-castes, indeed so low, according to the Hindu social system which is part of the Hindu religion, that if one of them happened to brush with the fringed end of his waist shawl a single apple or mango on a fruit stand meant for the trade of Brahmins, or high-castes, the entire contents of the store were con-sidered polluted and unclean and had to be thrown away; or if he happened to pass a barber shop patronized by high-castes and if his shadow fell on a razor, this razor could never be used again to shave the fat cheeks of a member of a higher social order. Others of them were water-carriers, artisans, and small shop keepers. Then there was a retired elephant driver, a small, bandy-legged, berry-brown man with flashing eyes and terrific bodily strength who, living on a small pension, used to boast about the glorious robes of honor that he wore when he was still in the service of His Highness the Nizam, Mahara-jah of Hyderabad, and told Jimmie long stories

—some of them, alas!, stretching the truth a little—about the great beast's extraordinary sagacity.

Still others were a small colony or tribe of jugglers from Matheran, settled in the north. During the cool season they used to go from city to city, from country fair to country fair, from bungalow to bungalow, performing their tricks. Jimmie would watch them when they practiced their craft. Some of them were very skilful. Almost entirely naked, and in the centre of an unfurnished room, they would cause a snake to appear and disappear, a mango tree to grow and bring forth fruit, or water to flow from an empty vase. Others would swallow sabres or play tricks with sharp knives. One of their most curious tricks was that of the basket and the child. A boy of seven or eight years, standing upright in the basket, would writhe in convulsions under the influence of plaintive, droning music, would double up, and suddenly disappear in the interior of the basket which was barely large enough to hold him. Scarcely was the boy inside, when the juggler would take a long, sharp sabre and pierce the basket in every direction, striking with all his might until, the bamboo giving way, the basket seemed completely flattened out, no longer able to hold anything. Then the music would begin again. A voice would come from very far, would seem to grow gradually nearer and nearer, at last issue from the broken basket itself. The basket would bloat and distend and, suddenly, the child would jump out.

But, whatever their trade, sweeper or water-carrier or juggler, they were all poor. Yet theirs was the tolerance and kindliness and charity of the poor the world over, and they gave Jimmie many a square meal, many a cooling drink, and occasionally—not often, for they had so very little themselves—a small piece of money.

So the years passed, and when he had reached his fifteenth year, early manhood came to him—sudden, and a little cruel, as it comes to those born in the tropics; and not long afterwards Mara, who had taken care of him to the best of her ability, died.

He was now alone.

There was in that far North-Indian town no American consul; nor, if there had been, would Jimmie have known what the term meant. There were of course a few European officials, servants of the British Raj. But to them, tanned by the sun, native in speech and garb, he was just a young Hindu, perhaps a half-caste, a Eurasian, if they stopped to consider the steely blue of his eyes; and, on his side, Jimmie seldom thought of them at all. To him a white man, a saheb, was a man who spoke broken and ridiculous Hindu, who grew angry on the slightest occasion, who got red in the face when you bothered him, and who once in a while, being a foreigner and therefore mad, could be persuaded to throw to the boys a gorgeous handful of tiny copper coins. His rare dealings with missionaries had taught him that they insisted on a great deal of bodily cleanliness and reading in large books, and so he avoided them—successfully, and aided and abetted by his two bosom friends, Mehmet Tugluk and Gandra Rai. Thus he lived the life of the Chawkpore slums, earning a precarious substance by helping Afgan and Jain, Tibetan and Pathan and Nepalese; a friend with all the brown and yellow world of the bazars; never really hungry because there was always enough currie and mutton and eggplant in the cookpots of the poor to feed one more mouth; picking up a strange dialect here, a strange custom there; and it was not often now that he recalled his father's injunction to remember that he was James Clinton Weatherby, American and gentleman, less often than he considered his father's last word of advice.

"Don't you ever wait for the next day! Think —think well—then do—at once!"

For in those days Jimmie never thought at all. He was too busy living, so why should he waste time in thinking? There were the streets, the

bazars, the sunshine, the motley throngs. There
were marriage feasts and burial feasts. There
was color and motion and fun. There were his
friends. There was always food and drink, always a few copper coins to be picked up.

Yet, still, was there deep in his consciousness
that curious longing for the north, that strange,
unreasoning homesickness for the snows and the
cool cleanliness of the snows; and he spent many
an evening in the *khan,* the caravanserai, amidst
the reek of the cookpots and the gurgling of the
pipes, listening to the gliding gossip of Tibetan
traders.

Even here, in the Indian slums, the quarters of
the Tibetans were considered—always by comparison—decidedly dirty and disorderly. For
these hillmen had the habit of removing such tri-
fling things as remains of food simply by throwing them away at random, regardless where they
fell or whom they happened to hit. They never
undressed, not even when they retired for the
night, and did not indulge in bedsteads nor in
bedclothes as Americans understand them, but
lay down anywhere, on the bare floor, and covered themselves with coarse skins and extra
wraps. For furniture they had only rudely-
hewn, low benches that served as tables, and logs
of wood that served as chairs. From pegs in
the wall hung bladders of butter which may have

been kept for years and that had accompanied the proud possessor through many miles of hard mountain climbing—a sort of haughty family heirloom,—and bits of smelly meat, yak-hair ropes, strings of rock-hard cheese, and on the top of some box would be a little shrine for the image of the household gods, besides a small religious picture and some charm against evil spirits.

Their food was plentiful if coarse, consisting of tea stewed up with butter, unleavened scones of wheat or barley meal eked out with the meal of roasted corn grains, a great mass of meat, potatoes, turnips and cabbage boiled up together in a large iron billypot, dried cheese as a relish, and on festive occasions a nibble at a bit of brown sugar.

Their table manners were as rough as their food, but their hospitality was splendid. Jimmie knew. He ate with them often enough, dipping his arms to the elbows in the large billypot and helping himself shamelessly to rich, fat pieces of mutton. He liked them, and they liked him.

There was chiefly one, a tall, raw-boned, lemon-colored merchant from the Chumbi valley, Ugyen Garyo by name, who would answer by the hour Jimmie's questions about this unknown land of Tibet which was frozen seven months in the year, which tried to keep all foreigners away from its threshold, which was ruled by savage, fighting, red-capped and yellow-capped monks and abbots and priests and, in far, mysterious Lhassa, by the great Dalai Lama himself, who claimed to be a fleshly incarnation of the Buddha, and whose divine names and many titles were uttered with devotion throughout Tibet, Mongolia, Ladak, and the Himalayan States down to Bothan, and from Lake Baikal in Russian Siberia to Western China.

"*Om ma-ni pad-me! Hung*: Hail, Jewel in the Lotus Flower!"   Ugyen Garyo exclaimed devoutly, clicking his prayer wheel. "He is the *Gyal-wa*—the Precious Protector! The *Kyah-gon-Rim-po-che*—the   Ever-Victorious   Lord! is the *Gyat-sho*—The Vast as the Ocean!"

"What does he look like?" asked Jimmie, excitedly.

"The sun is his face, and the moon, and the thousand-thousand stars!"

"Have you ever seen him?"

"I have kissed his shadow—in sign of devotion —twice!"

"I'd love to see him, too!" said Jimmie. "Take me with you when you go home!"

"No!"

"I thought we were friends!"

"We are," smiled the Tibetan, "the best in the world, but——"

"No!"   Ugyen Garyo shook his head.   "It is not permitted."

"Why not?"

"Keep to your side of the border.   We of the north do not like foreigners, nor their speech, nor their ways, nor their customs, nor their faces. *Om ma-ni pad-me! Hung!*—Hail, Jewel in the Lotus Flower!"   Again he clicked his wooden prayer wheel, filled with red paper prayers.

Jimmie smiled.

"Ugyen Garyo!" he said after a pause.

"Well, little heathen?"

"I have heard—things——"

"Where?"

"In the bazars."

"Doubtless.   The bazars are filled with leaky tongues and lying throats."

"Leaky tongues?   Yes!   But not all throats lie—at least—" Jimmie added after considering —"they do not lie always.   For instance——"

"For instance—?"   The Tibetan looked up from beneath heavy, opium-reddened eyelids.

"I have heard about certain sahebs, certain white men, who, remembering the pact of peace and trade between the British Raj and the Dalai Lama, have begun trading into the north.   I have heard that Southern Tibet is as full of the sahebs' agents as an old coat is of vermin.   I have heard that the agents are all the way up the

Chumbi valley, that they have dealings even with the red-capped and the yellow-capped priests— that——"

"*Om ma-ni pad-me! Hung!*" interrupted the Tibetan, passionlessly. "Have you ever heard about the fleet horse and its tail?"

"Well?"

"Even the fleetest horse can't escape its tail, little heathen!"

"A threat?" laughed Jimmie.

"No, little heathen! A prophecy! Here—" hospitably—"dip your hands into the mutton stew! Fat mutton flavored with honey and wild herbs! Help yourself! Fill your little gullet! *Om ma-ni pad-me! Hung!*"

It was not many days after his conversation with Ugyen Garyo that Jimmie, for the first time with growing consciousness of what the words signified, declared aloud that he was James Clinton Weatherby, American and gentleman, and it happened at the occasion of a *mela,* a country fair, given on the outskirts of Chawkpore. He went there early, accompanied by his friends Mehmet Tugluk and Gandra Rai, and it seemed that all the countryside for many a mile was going to the fair. The road was thronged with foot passengers, with horsemen, with Moslems and Hindus and a few Europeans, with all kinds of vehicles, with an occasional camel or elephant.

The rich were as eager as the poor to take part in the gaiety of the fair, the circus of India, and —had Jimmie only known it—it was just the sort of affair, a few climatic and linguistic differences apart, which his father had often seen and enjoyed when he had been a child, up New York state where he came from.

Yes—questions of language and color and dress apart, there were here the same shouts, the same spielers, the same grotesque advertisements, the same lollypop and lemonade stalls—and, perhaps, the same confidence men and swindlers and thimble-riggers waiting for the long-suffering "rube"—showing that, at least, in this respect, the East is surprisingly like the West.

The three friends pushed along with the crowd. The scene was one of jollity. Tents and ambulant coffee-houses were filled with men and women in their holiday best, listening to singers and musicians, smoking and chatting, and looking at jugglers, sword-twirlers, snake-charmers, and dancing boys in women's attire. There were eating-stalls, and Punch-and-Judy shows, and candy-booths filled with the greasy sweets which delight the palate of the Indian.

There were of course the many cries of the *mela.*

"Sweet water here!" would come the cry of the lemonade seller as he clanked his metal cups

together, while the vendor of parched grain, rat-
tling the wares in his basket, would chime in with:
"O chick pease! O pips! To sharpen they
teeth—thy stomach—thy mind!"

"Out of the way—and say 'There is but One
God!' ", came the long, quivering shout of the
Moslem water-carrier, carrying the luke-warm
fluid in a goat's-skin bag, immensely heavy, fit
burden for a buffalo.

"My supper is in Allah's hands! My supper
is in Allah's hands! Whatever thou givest, that
will return to thee through Allah!" whined an
old vagrant whose wallet perhaps contained more
provision than the basket of many a respectable
shop-keeper.

"The grave is darkness, and good deeds are
its lamps," chanted a blind beggar woman, rap-
ping two sticks together.

"In thy protection! In thy protection!" a
peasant implored a Sikh policeman who was flog-
ging him toward the station-house.

"O Calamity! O Shame! O Dragon-Tooth!
O Accursed and very unbeautiful Duck-Egg!"
shrieked a woman, as she yanked her tiny pert-
eyed girl-child from beneath the crimson-paper
partition of a sugar-candy booth. The next moment she fondled her and kissed her. "O Peace
of my Soul!" she cooed. "O Chief Pride of Thy
Father's house—though a girl!"

A high-caste Hindu, fat and statuesque and haughty, moved through the crowd in state, preceded by half a dozen turbaned, stalwart henchmen, who were shouting insulting and defying words at everybody, and belabored with a beautiful, democratic impartiality the backs and things of merchants and peasants, Moslems and Hindus, high-castes and low-castes alike.

"O thy right!" they yelled as they brought down their long, brass-tipped staves, "O thy left! O thy face! O thy heel!"—smiting the swing of their sticks to the part of Oriental anatomy which they were striking. "O thy back, thy back, thy back! Give way, ignoble and unmentionable ones!"

Friend would meet friend and greet each other with all the extravagance of the East, throwing themselves upon each other's breasts, placing right arm over left shoulder, squeezing like wrestlers, with intermittent hugs and caresses, then laying cheek delicately against cheek and flat palm against palm, at the same time making the loud, smacking noise of many kisses in the air.

Mild-mannered, suave, and sleepy-eyed, they would burst into torrents of rage at the next moment because of some fancied insult. Their nostrils would quiver, and they would become furious as Bengal tigers. Then would come streams of abuse, carefully chosen phrases of that picturesque vituperation in which the Orient excels.

"Owl! Donkey! Christian! Leper! Drunkard! Lizard-eating, low-caste sweeper bereft of gratitude, understanding, and all the decencies!" This from an elderly Hindu whose carefully trimmed, white beard gave him an aspect of patriarchal holiness in ridiculous contrast with the foul invective which he was using. "Unclean and swinish foreigner!"—to a Moslem— "Eater of holy cows! May thy countenance be cold! May thou be born for a thousand lives in ·the bodies of crawling, venomous insects!"

Came the reply courteous:

"Basest of hyenas! Father of three thousand and three piglings! Goat! Father of little goats! Truly I shall torture thee the torture of the oil, the torture of the peg, the torture of the water! By Allah and by Allah—and again by Allah!"

Then the final retort, drawling, slow-voiced, but containing all the venom of India:

"Ho! Thy aunt had no nose!"

And, at last, a physical assault, an exchange of blows, hearty on the Moslem's and rather weak on the Hindu's side, until the laughing, spitting Sikh policeman in the scarlet tunic of the British Raj separated them and cuffed both Hindu and Moslem with cheerfully democratic impartiality.

It seemed as if all India had come to the *mela,* as if all the traders and artisans of many races who lived about the Chawkpore district, some settled there for good, others for the season's trade and gains, had closed shops and warehouses to celebrate.

For there were Babus from Bengal, black and ungainly and oily, shuffling along on patent-leather pumps. There were bearded Rajputs, wide-shouldered, 'wide-stepping. There were thick-chested bow-legged men from the Punjaub, furtive-stepping men from the Madras Presidency, ruffianly Afghan caravanmen who picked fights wherever they went, and here and there a massive Sikh, conspicuous because of his blue-checkered turban and the bit of cut steel which glimmered in its heavy folds.

There were yellow-faced Tibetan hillmen who still seemed scented with the acrid herbs of the mountains and who looked about them with an odd mixture of wonder and contempt. There were desertmen from Bikaneer, with vicious eyes, frowning brows, coarse, bushy hair burned rust-red by the sun, and the jaws bandaged after the manner of the desert. There were men from Hyderabad, mounted on lean, well-bred ponies, riding as hard as Wyoming cowboys, with a complete disregard for foot passengers.

It was not long before Jimmie was separated in the crowd from his two friends, but he pushed along, laughing, swapping jokes and curses and comments with the swaying, jostling throng in Indi and Urdi and Tibetan, thoroughly enjoying the riot and the tumult of it all.

He loved the open-air Punch-and-Judy shows. The latter are to the masses of Hindu humanity what theatres, motion pictures, funny papers, Sunday newspaper comic supplements, and—last not least—political pamphlets and stump speeches mean to the American crowds. For not only do the gawky, lanky marionettes portray comedies and dramas of Hindu life, but also—under the noses of the British police, and unimpeachable since no word is spoken—do they picture, caricature, and flay whatever fault the people may have to find with the Raj, the British-Indian government. Just as in the old Italian Punch-and-Judy show there is always a policeman who is the villain and who finally gets knocked on the head by brave Harlequin's bladder-sausage, so in the Indian marionette theatre the villain is usually an Englishman, easily discernible by the clumsy doll's exaggerated beak of a nose, yellow straw hair, round, blue pebbles stuck in for eyes, short red coat and tight trousers—and howls of laughter or cries of rage at the imitation "saheb's"

comic or brutal actions, and at last a storm of
applause when the brave Hindu Harlequin chops
off his head with a papier-maché scimitar.

And Jimmie laughed, raged, and applauded
with the best of them.   He had never been over-
fond of "sahebs."

Of. course religion is an essential of Hindu
life.   The many gods of their faith seem never
far away; and, chiefly since it was near the date
of the great Doorgha-Puja festival, the celebra-
tion of that day when Pravati, the god Shiva's
consort, because he killed the giant Doorgha who
had threatened the gods with destruction, had
assumed the giant's name in token of triumph and
was ever after herself known as Doorgha, there
were many Brahmin priests, with scarlet caste
marks on their foreheads, in the crowd, gathering listeners around them and reciting the chap-
ters of the Vedas, the holy scriptures of the
Hindus, which speak of the wondrous happening.
Here and there, as Jimmie pushed through the
throng, he could hear the ancient Sanskrit text
declared with the correct scansion and rhythm
of the ritual—rising and falling, gaining strength
and sweep, then dying in a thin, quavery falsetto;

"—and first Pravati sent Kalavatri, the Black
Knight, to slay the giant and to restore everything
to the appointed order.   But Kalavatri——"

"Ho!   The blessed miracle!" shouted the

crowd, and Jimmie shouted with the best of them.

On another corner a Brahmin on whose forehead was a caste-mark of diagonal stripes of black and white wax was chanting the praises of Ganesha, the elephant-headed god, first-born of the sons of Shiva and Doorgha.

"Praise to thee!" chanted the priest. "Propitious One, son of Shava and Doorgha! Thou art manifestly the Truth! Thou art doubtless the Creator, Preserver, and Destroyer! Thou art the Supreme Being, the King, the Eternal Spirit! We acknowledge thy Divinity, O Ekedanta, and we meditate on thy Countenance!"

On the next corner a purple-marked priest was holding a sort of opposition revival. For he was droning the praises of the second son of Doorgha, of Kratikeya, God of War, telling to all the world how he was born on the banks of the Ganges to slay the evil demon Tarika.

The people listened to the oft-told tale. A gaunt, red-turbaned Punjaubi fell flat on his face, overcome by religious frenzy.

"*Wahuwa!*" he screamed, and there was foam on his lips. "*Wahuwa!* Oh—the blessed miracle!"

The crowd pressed in, to help the Punjabi to his feet, to restore him, Jimmie amongst them. He pushed and pulled, partly out of curiosity, partly out of sympathy, when suddenly he felt a hand taking him by the collar and jerking him backward.

He looked up and around, ready to protest, to fight, and saw that his assailant was a white boy of about his own age, evidently English.

"Hey there!" Jimmie exclaimed in English. "Stop that, will you?"

Again the other jerked him back. "Out of my way! I want to see!"

"Here—you—" in moments of excitement and stress Jimmie's English was liable to become sketchy—"What you mean by——"

"Out of my way!" the other repeated, pushing Jimmie to one side; then, as the latter's fist clenched while a dancing high-light eddied up in his eyes: "Don't you dare touch me, you nigger!"

Be it mentioned in passing that in India the word "nigger" has not the meaning which it has in America; it is not a vulgar term for "negro." It is simply an appellation given by foolish Europeans to natives—doubly foolish, since a good half of the latter are quite as light-skinned as the average European while millions of them, chiefly those of Persian, Central Asian, and Hindu-Aryan blood, are in fact much fairer. But the meaning of the word is insulting. And Jimmie flushed crimson.

It was then that he remembered his father's words.   But this time he pronounced them consciously challengingly:

"I am James Clinton Weatherby!   I'm not a nigger!"

"All right, all right.   You're not.   But you're a Hindu, anyway!

"No!"

"Yes!"

"I am an American and a gentleman—I tell you my name is James Clinton Weatherby——"

"Oh—is it?   Well, whatever it is, take my advice and keep out of the way—you——"

Came an insulting word, and the very next moment Jimmie, who had won his spurs in many a rough-and-tumble fight with ruffianly Afghan and Pathan boys in the bazars, waded in.   Nor did he adhere strictly to the gentlemanly rules of combat laid down by the late Marquis of Queensberry.   His methods were more to the point, more primitive, and also more effective, with the result that, inside of a minute and a half, the English boy lay prone on the ground, crying with rage and pain—but with yet another result which was rather more disastrous for the victor.

For a Sikh policeman hustled through the crowd, took Jimmie by the scruff of the neck, dragged him away, screaming and kicking and biting, and deposited him, twenty minutes later, in front of a choleric, red-faced British magistrate, with the charge:

"He struck young Dalton saheb, the son of Sir James Dalton, the resident commissioner saheb!"

"Oh—he did, did he?"   The magistrate turned to Jimmie.   "Well?   What have you to say for yourself, my lad?"

"I——"

"Did you do it?"

·"Yes!" said Jimmie defiantly.   "And I'll do it again——"

"Nice young rebel, hey?"

"He called me——"

"Saheb!" the policeman interfered, talking volubly, and the magistrate inclined his head.

"Fifty rupees fine!" came his draconic judgment.   "Or three days in jail!   Next case!"

"He called me nigger!" shouted Jimmie, indignant.   "Then he called me Hindu!   Then he insulted me!   And I am James Clinton Weatherby! I am an American and a gentleman!"

"Ripping imagination!" commented the magistrate.   "Colossal corker of a wopper!   Truly Oriental!   Well—can you pay the fine?   Fifty rupees?   Of course not!   Hey there—" turning to a court attendant—"Churda Singh?"

"Yes, saheb?"

A Sikh policeman dragged him away

"Off to jail with him! Next case!" He pounded the table.

So off to jail went Jimmie, still protesting vociferously that he was in the right, that he was James Clinton Weatherby, American and gentleman, and was put behind the locked door of a prison cell.

He was furious with rage. His fists clenched until the knuckles stretched white. His blue eyes blazed. He felt the injustice of the sentence keenly, perhaps with a racial, non-thinking, instinctive memory of his ancestors who had gone to America because of that same principle. But what hurt him most was the idea that here he would have to spend three days in jail, away from the streets and bazars, the sun and the motley crowds which he loved. Fifty rupees fine! There was the alternative. Why, he said to himself, there was not that much cash in the whole of the Kashmiri bazar even if all his friends, Afghan mutton-butcher and Hindu sweeper, Nepalese coppersmith and Tibetan merchant, chipped in to make up the total. He was in a rage, pacing up and down, impatiently watching the minutes stretching out in a silent, maddening, creaking procession. The jailer came in a few minutes later with a jug of water. He was a brown-faced, agate-eyed Babu, very fat and oily and clad in white gauze which, considering his fantastic bodily contours, gave him a decidedly grotesque appearance. Jimmie tried to talk to him; but the man shook his head.

"Against regulation number fifteen, paragraph three, to talk to prisoners," he replied, and left the cell.

Half an hour later he returned with a basket. It was evident to Jimmie that there was no hope left for him, that he would have to spend the night here—three nights in fact. He wondered if some of his native friends would be allowed to visit him. So again he turned to the Babu jailer with a question; again the latter shook his head, remaining silent.

Then Jimmie grew angry.

"Look here, son of a pig!" he cried. "Answer my question, or I'll throw this chair at you!"

The Babus smiled patiently.

"Speaking in my official capacity," he said, with the precise deliberation of a phonograph, "I will state that it is against the law to throw chairs or other hard substances at the heads of members of the Indian judiciary. Yes—against the law! See Bengal Criminal code, volume three, chapter five, paragraph fifteen, entitled 'Interference with Government Officials in the Execution of their Duties.' See also chapter seven, paragraph eight, entitled 'Assault with Intent to Kill!' Please—do not throw the chair!"

And the man was serious, utterly serious.   So Jimmie gave him up after that and, finally, fell into uneasy sleep.

It did not seem more than ten minutes later when the door opened and the jailer came in again.

"A saheb to see you," he announced.

"Who?" asked Jimmie astonished.

"I!" said a voice from the door, as a tall, lean man entered, grey-haired, clean-shaven, sharp-featured, with a high nose, thin lips, and a humorous twinkle in his blue eyes.   He pulled out a cigar, lit it, took out another one and tossed it to the Babu with instructions to smoke it outside, then turned to Jimmie.

"So you are James Clinton Weatherby?" he asked.

"I am!   How do you know?"

"Can't help knowing it!   Heard you shout it loud enough and often enough.   I was in the courtroom, you see, waiting to be witness—clerk of mine swiped some cash.   American, are you? White?"

"I am!"

"Hm!"   Coolly the newcomer walked up to Jimmie and pulled open his ragged shirt.   "Sure enough—quite white—even if you are a little grimy.   Born here?"

"Yes."

"Always lived here?"

"But——"

"What business is it of mine? Oh—not a bit! Still—mind answering? Always lived here?"

"Yes."

"Good enough. I am Rankin—Monro W. Rankin. I'm an American, too. Shake, boy!"

They shook hands.

"Fifty rupees fine, eh?" continued the man. "All right. I'll pay it for you."

Jimmie smiled. He did not show the slightest hesitancy in accepting. He liked the other, and he felt instinctively that the feeling was mutual.

"Thank you," he said.

"Good names," went on Rankin, "you're sporting. Both the Clinton and the Weatherby."

"So my father told me."

"Where did he come from? New England, I take it—or perhaps up-state New York?"

"I don't know."

"I'm from San Francisco myself. Heard of her, haven't you?"

"No!"

"Well—I'll be darned. Still—she's a peach of a burg—take it from me, boy—and I don't care *what* they say in Los Angeles!"

Rankin laughed, and for some reason Jimmie joined in the laugh. He liked the other better and better. He thanked him again, a few minutes later, when his fine had been paid and he walked down the street by the side of 'his new-found friend.

At the corner Rankin extended his hand.

"I hope I'll see you when I get back."

"Where are you going?"

"Up north. To Tibet. Up the Chumbi val-ley a ways!"

Jimmie's eyes glistened. "To—to Tibet?" he stammered.

"Sure enough. I am chief inspector of the Central Asian Chartered Company for the Hima-layan district. Heard of the C. A. C. C., haven't you?"

It was, in fact, the same Central Asian Char-tered Company, called the C. A. C. C. lovingly and for short by its many employees, to which Jim-mie had referred in his conversation with Uryen Garyo, the Tibetan trader. Backed by powerful American, English and Dutch capital, its head-quarters in a grey old continental metropolis, with a king for chief stockholder, a prime minister for president, a bishop for secretary, a Hebrew banker with a historic name for treasurer, allied to grant banks in Paris, London, Chicago, New York, and Brussels, it held almost imperial sway in Central Asia, from Pekin to Kazan, from the shores of Lake Baikal to the Mountains of the

Moon.   Its agents and factors, its explorers and concession hunters and inspectors and special investigators were the reckless spirits of all the world, keen, clever, often unscrupulous; shrewd, down-east Yankees, Brazilian Jews, Portuguese half-castes, Cockneys, Welshmen, Armenians, Arabs, and Glasgow Scots.   It was only of late that, relying on the treaty between the Dalai Lama of Lhassa and the British Raj, they had commenced trading into Tibet, and it was an admitted fact throughout the bazars of the Indian border towns that, in spite of the treaty, the Dalai Lama had decided to evade its clauses, to keep his country inviolate from foreign intercourse as it had been in the past centuries.   It was going to be a tug-of-war between the shrewdness of the Tibetan priest-kings and that of the C. A. C. C., and here this lean, smiling American was going up the Chumbi valley as chief inspector —up to the North, the cool, clean snows of the hills—up to Tibet!

"Please!" cried Jimmie suddenly.   "Take me along, won't you?"

"You're crazy, boy!   Stay home and play baseball or whatever they do play hereabouts!"

"No, no!   I want to go!   Please take me!"

"Don't be silly!"

"I *want* to go!" insisted Jimmie.

"Sure   enough.   But—why,   boy—you   know

nothing of business—you know—" Rankin laughed, and lit another cigar—"What *do* you know?"

And then Jimmie had an inspiration.

"I know Tibetan!" he replied. "I know two or three of the hill dialects!"

Rankin stood still. He whistled through his teeth.

"Oh—you do, do you?" he demanded, interested.

"Yes."

"Well, well, well! That's a horse of a different complexion altogether!" He studied Jimmie's face, long, sharply, scrutinizingly. "James Clinton Weatherby, eh? An American, eh? Speaks Hindu and Tibetan and what-not? By jimmini—" he laughed—"I go you, boy! You're engaged!"

"When do we start?"

"This afternoon!" Rankin smiled. "I guess it won't take you long to pack?"

Jimmie pointed at his ragged native garb.

"I'm packed now!" he replied.

CHAPTER II

IT was thus that, early the next day, Rankin
and Jimmie stepped out of the train at Sili-
guri, followed by a fur-capped, broad-shouldered
Afghan mountaineer by the name of Ghula Khan
—name which he changed frequently and at will
—who formerly had dealt with stallions out of
Kabul into Peshawur, with wretched off-color
emeralds, also with striped Bokhariot belts, salt,
onyx-eyed Persian kittens, and several unclassified
items of Central Asian merchandise, amongst
them guns and ammunition to marauding border
Pathans, and who recently had decided that India
was not a safe place for him. So thanks to a ruffianly and voluble perseverance, he had enrolled
himself under the banner of the C. A. C. C., as
body guard to Mr. Monro W. Rankin.

His first encounter with Jimmie had been quite
typical of both.

"Boy!" the Afghan had said, passionlessly, without special reason or provocation. "Thou art an exceedingly small and unbeautiful flea!"

"But I can bite!"

"Ha! Ho!" the Afghan had laughed, with something akin to respect. "Good-by Beelzebub, Father of Lies!"

But more of Ghula Khan and his sudden decision that India was not for him hereafter.

For the moment, and for many a moment, many an hour, he was busy, with the help of Jimmie and of a few Tibetan coolies recruited on the spot, sorting the little hills of piled-up stores which they needed for their journey; grain and flour, sugar, salt, medicines, boxes of provisions, brandy, bundles of clothing, saddles and riding-gear. It was early afternoon before they were ready to travel. They were now warmly dressed in sheepskin coats with long sleeves, Balaklava caps tied round their chins with woolen scarves, thick fur gloves, quilted overalls, lambswool vests, boots of fur-lined felt reaching to the knees, and yellow goggles against snow blindness. And so, two days later, while the coolies panted and puffed, while the horses and mules squealed and kicked and bucked, they struggled slowly, painfully, patiently, up the steep, winding staircase of the Himalayas, zigzagging up the spurs of the higher ranges, passing through the cooler zones of dwarf oak and chestnut and maple and elm, with undergrowths of raspberry and barberry, out into the open, snow-flecked pine forest below the shoulder of Lingtu Mountain.

The hardest traveling of this part of their journey was through a deep-slit gorge where a turbulent river pierced the rocks. It is very well named "The Cleft of the Winds" by the Lepcha natives, for through it pours an immense, ceaseless stream of mist and rushing, howling wind, as though through a mighty chimney, blowing a gale down the valley in day time and up at it at night.

It frightened Jimmie a little; made him long a little for the comfort of the Chawkpore streets. And the Afghan laughed at him mockingly.

"Ho!" he commented. "The more the tiger gets away from home, the more he becomes a lamb, eh?"

And it is saying a lot for the hardness of the journey to relate that Jimmie was rather slow and rather clumsy in his repartee:

"*Wah!* Thou art a scabbard without the sword. Why should I fear thee, father of seventy-seven piglings?"

But in spite of the clumsiness of the insult, the Afghan became angry and was about to raise a menacing fist when, suddenly, he noticed that Jimmie had turned pale—nor pale with fear, the mountaineer could tell—and trembling as if with ague.

"What is the matter, young wart on the devil's nose?" he asked.

"I feel chilly," replied Jimmie.

"Chilly—in this heat? A touch of fever—I am sure."

And so it was; and the American dosed him with quinine, and took the same precaution with regard to the Afghan and to himself.

The country here was indeed highly malarial, not only because of the swarms of great mosquitoes, but because the wind that rushed day and night through the gorge is laden with miasmic exhalations of the rank, tropical jungle of the other side.

They stopped for half an hour until Jimmie had overcome his fever fit, and then went on.

Though unhealthy and rough, the gorge was grandly beautiful. The river's low banks and islets were covered by a dense and almost impenetrable virgin forest in whose deep, leafy recesses lurked almost every kind of wild beast, from tiger downwards, as well as the game on which they preyed.

Beyond the gorge they struck a rich, lush land where here and there along the road, peeped up the picturesque huts of the sturdy hill people who,

braving the rough trip and the unhealthiness of
the gorge, come here every year for a few weeks
to trade, or to pick up livelihood as wood cutters.
Most of them were immigrants from the adjoin-
ing hills of Nepal; but there were also some
traders from Tibet, accompanied by huge mastiffs
and leading shaggy ponies laden with a little wool
which they had managed to smuggle in from the
Forbidden Land. And Jimmie met one or two
old friends amongst them—men with whom he
had broken bread and tasted salt in the Chawkpore caravanserais.

They greeted him with good-humored rough-
ness.

"Whither away, O small shadow of nothing at
all?"

"To thine own country—to Tibet, O noseless
one!" came Jimmie's laughing reply, and then a
good-natured wink and comment that "the cock
leaves home for seven days, and returns a peacock."

All in all, Jimmie enjoyed himself thoroughly,
although the next day the road became rougher
and more lonely.

They met now few people; occasionally a British outpost, in the brown of Sikh soldiery, the red
of the English, or the rifle-green of the Goorkha
regiments, who examined their passports, a few
Tibetan and Nepalese traders plodding down into

the plains, panting under heavy loads and once, near Ringo, a gaunt yellow-cap Lamaist priest who cursed them roundly and picturesquely and threatened them with the vengeance of all the Tibetan gods for defiling the Forbidden Land.

Up they went, beyond the Tibetan frontier, advancing, fifteen thousand feet high, through the ragged cleft of the Jelep Pass, swept by a merciless ice blast which cut through the thickest garments like a knife, which snatched away their breath, and which forced them, oppressed by the rarefied air, to a stop for rest every few yards.

That night they rested on the banks of a frozen mountain torrent, close to a blazing fire of pine logs.   But the cold was withering; a cup of tea transformed itself into a dirty-brown lump of ice before they had time to raise it to their lips and drink it; and Jimmie suffered intensely.   He longed for the warm, cozy reek of the Chawkpore bazars.

Ghula Khan, who had been up this way before many a time, acted as guide, and Rankin had left a chart of their proposed route in the office of the North-Indian headquarters of the C. A. C. C. at Darjeeling, southwest of the Jelep Pass, so that he could keep in touch with his people and receive news from them.   And news reached him late that night when a runner joined them, traveling rapidly through the snow that had begun coming down in a soft whirl.   He introduced himself as Offan Kharo, a native of the small State, Sikhim, which under British protection borders Tibet. He handed his credentials to Rankin, squatted down close to the fire, and fell to talking in English, in an undertone.

Jimmie, half asleep, half frozen, yet keenly interested, caught a word here and there, heard Rankin ask sharp questions and the Afghan, too, join in the conversation.   All three seemed excited, talking in tense whispers, then Ghula's Khan's voice boomed out strongly:

"Perhaps, Rankin saheb, the mountains have eaten them up."

"Don't be an ass!" laughed the American. "Mountains aren't cannibals——"

"But the people of the mountains——"

"Aren't cannibals either."

"The fact remains, saheb, that they have disappeared—haven't they, Offan Kharo?"

The latter inclined his head.

"Yes," he said, "all three of them.   Murdered, I have no doubt."

"But—by whom?" demanded Rankin.

"By the Tibetans, of course."

"No, no—they are a friendly lot, take them all in all."

"But the priests, the yellow-caps and red-caps!"

exclaimed the Afghan. "They may have given orders!"

"No," said the American, "there is our treaty with the Dalai Lama."

"I have heard of treaties being broken."

"Sure enough, here as well as in Europe. Scraps of paper, eh?"

"Exactly!" agreed Ghula Khan.

"On the other hand," went on Rankin, "the C. A. C. C. made a little private compact with the Tashi Lama, the Lamaist high priest at Tashil-humpo. His Holiness—if that's the correct name to give him—gave a most sacred oath on a whole stack of Tibetan equivalent for Bibles, that the lives of our agents would be safe!"

"Did he really give such an oath?" asked the man from Sikhim.

"Sure enough!"

"Bazar talk!" interjected Ghula Khan. "I do not believe it."

"You can believe it all right, all right!" smiled the American. "The old bird came down to Darjeeling. I interviewed him myself."

"Oh—?" The Afghan whistled through his teeth. "Did you ask him to come down and give the oath?"

"No. He came of his own free will!"

"Own free will? Pah!" laughed the Afghan.

"There is only one will in Tibet—and that is the will of the Dalai Lama, up in Lhassa! If he gave the oath, he was ordered to give it—and there was a reason for it!"

"But he did give it. There's the long and short of it. What do you think, Offan Kharo?"

The latter shook his head.

"Saheb," he said, "the Tashi Lama would not break his oath. He is as important in Western Tibet as the Dalai Lama is in the whole of the Forbidden Land. He too is said to be an earthly incarnation of Srongtsan Gamp himself who, in his turn, was an incarnation of the Compassionate Spirit of the Mountain—almost a Buddha."

"Words, words!" commented Rankin. "Words that have no meaning for me. I'm a business man, first, last, and all the time. You said that the Tashi Lama would not break his oath?"

"Yes, saheb. And yet—" he shrugged his shoulders.

"And yet," the Afghan took up the sentence, with a hard, dry laugh, "it seems that three of the C. A. C. C. agents have disappeared."

"Yes," said Offan Kharo, "all the three agents of the company! Disappeared completely, leaving no trace! That's why I hastened after you from Darjeeling, saheb, to give the news."

"What does headquarters think of it?" demanded the American.

"They have started investigating.   As soon as they find trace, they will communicate with you by runner——"

"As soon as they find trace!" echoed Ghula Khan mockingly.   "I'd as soon try and measure the ocean's depth with a jackal's tail—as soon try and catch the seven winds of heaven with a rope made of tortoise-hair!   Allah!   I know these Tibetans!   Allah's curse on them all!"

"Then why did you insist on accompanying me?" asked the American, with a wink.

"Because," replied the Afghan, winking back shamelessly, "there are moments when even a Tibetan's company is preferable to that of the British Raj!   Because there are moments when a man like myself is—ah—careless!"

"In the meantime," went on the man from Sikhim, "headquarters beg you to be careful, saheb.   Wait in Ya-tung until you hear from us."

"All right, old man.   I'll do my best."

"Mr. Rankin!" cut in Jimmie, sitting up.

"Hullo," the other laughed.   "Another county heard from?   Been awake and listening, eh?"

"I couldn't help myself.   And—I want to tell you something——"

"Well?   What has our youngest Tibetan authority to contribute to the gaiety of nations?"

"I've a friend, a Tibetan trader—Ugyen Garyo——"

"A powerful trader up Chumbi way," interposed the runner.

"He told me—oh—things, when I mentioned to him that the sahebs are trading with Tibet."

"What exactly did he say, Jimmie?"

"That even the fleetest horse cannot escape its own tail!"

Rankin laughed.

"I wish you Orientals wouldn't waste so much time coining metaphors and epigrams," he commented, "and stick a little more closely to business. It'd be better all around. Good night, all!" And he rolled himself in his fur-lined blanket and dropped off to sleep.

They were on the march again by day-break, the runner taking the southern trail and returning post-haste to headquarters, while the others descended into the Chumbi valley, down through a forest of silver firs, crossing frozen rivers which were like sloping sheets of ice, literal "death-slides" where the horses, and even the mules slid at every step, through a land where everything was frozen up tight, and no signs of life anywhere except an occasional flight of snow-pigeons winging it for some sunnier, thawing spot, and once— "ill omen!" the Afghan said, rapidly snapping his fingers to ward off the little devils of misfortune —a large, red-necked vulture, picking at the carcass of a yak and making unseemly noises in his naked, mangy throat as the little caravan came into sight. East and west the upper ranges, over twenty thousand feet above the level of the sea, gleamed upon them with sharp, white fangs, while, yet farther away, towered the dark ramparts of the Himalayan Divide.

Here the road was very dangerous, chiefly where it crossed the numerous landslips and ledges of gravel banks undermined below by the gigantic, snow-fed river floods. Once or twice Jimmie became dizzy, and looking over the edges of dangerous precipices, he saw frequent evidence of animals—even of human beings—who had fallen, had died, and shuddered a little as he saw the great, carrion-fed vultures gathering round the grisly remains.

As they descended a little more into the valley, the snows gradually began to thaw and here and there they crossed a meadow, sprinkled with the frosted remains of wild-flowers, primulas and celandines and wood-sorrel, while farther on there was an undulating stretch of alpine pasture studded with junipers and rhododendrons where long-haired yaks were grazing peacefully, indifferent to the biting cold; and so, finally, after a day's journey, another night spent close to a blazing fire, they reached the first Tibetan settlement at Ya-tung, early the following morning.

It was not a very important place, and so the

C. A. C. C. had never troubled to establish an agency there. But, immediately upon their arrival, the governor of the valley, the *Depon* to call him by his Tibetan title, a good-looking youngish man by the name of Kyu-go rode up in his rough little hill pony to meet them.

He and Rankin knew each other, and the latter greeted him heartily, in that friendly, rather careless and entirely good-natured manner which, typically American and not as highly polished as the European, is also less insincere than the latter and is perhaps—taken all round—one of the chief reasons why the average Asiatic prefers the American to the European. After all, human nature is the same the world over, be it black or brown or white or piebald, and there is no quality in ordinary human intercourse quite as conducive to friendship and easy relation as ordinary kindliness.

Once, during the journey, Rankin had said so to Jimmie.

"Don't you see, boy?" he had explained. "It's so darned hard to be unfriendly—isn't it?"

He showed it now.

"Glad to see you, old man!" He shook hands with the other.

The Tibetan laughed.

"Not half as glad as I am," he replied.

"What are you doing in this burg?" continued

the American.   "I thought you live at Phari fort,
up the valley?"

The Tibetan coughed.   He seemed a little embarrassed.

"Well—?" went on Rankin, "what's the matter?   Am I wrong?   Aren't you supposed to live
at Phari fort?"

"Yes, my friend."

"Don't be so mysterious!   What *is* the matter?"

"I came down to meet you as soon as I heard
that you had crossed the border."

"I call that hospitable.   Thanks."

"Rankin saheb," the other cut in, "I am a friend
of yours."

"You bet!   And that goes double.   Remember that little private party you and I had last
time you were in Darjeeling—when I taught you
the great American game of poker?"

"Yes.   And I also remember that you are an
excellent player.   You—" the *Depon* coughed—
"you know when you are beaten—you do not try
to bet an impossible hand, if I recall rightly——"

"Meaning what, old man?"

"Rankin saheb," the other continued, speaking
slowly, courteously, but with a vibrant earnestness
of purpose, "will you take my advice?"

"You bet—if it's good advice."

"It is, saheb!"

"All right. Go ahead and shoot, old son!"

The Tibetan hesitated a little. There was no doubt that he was embarrassed, even a little frightened. Nor was there a doubt, when he spoke a moment later, that he was utterly sincere.

"Go back, my friend," he said.

"What?" came Rankin's astonished rejoinder.

The Tibetan pointed south, toward India, where the peaks and crags of the Himalayas soared up like eager lances.

"Go back, my friend," he repeated, his voice rising an octave.

"Joshing, aren't you, old man?"

"No! Take my advice! Go back!"

"What do you mean—go back? Go back—where?"

"To your side of the border!"

"If so, why so?"

"Because Srongtsan Gampo, the Compassionate Spirit of the Mountains, is angry! Srongtsan Gampo has sent a message! *Om ma-ni pad-me! Hung!* Go back!"

The American shook his head. "Here's that Srongtsan—whatd'ye call him again. Never met the gentleman as far as I know. Look here, old son——"

"Saheb," interrupted the Tibetan, "consider that I have given fair warning—because we are friends, you and I."

"Say—would you mind being a little more explicit?" asked Rankin.

The other looked warily over his shoulder. Ya-tung was only a very small settlement, not more than twenty or thirty houses, low-roofed windowless huts rather, built of blackish-purple peat sods and huddled together like shivering oxen. A handful of the inhabitants, short, squat, red-faced Tibetans clad in felt and furs, were in the street, occasionally bowing and putting out their tongues, which is the respectful salutation of these parts. They appeared friendly enough beneath their dirt, and some even had already approached the caravan to haggle with Jimmie, Ghula Khan, and the coolies over food. They brought what they had, frozen yak-meat and butter and dried milk balls, anxious to exchange it for a few grains of rice, the greatest culinary luxury north of the passes.

The *Depon* looked at them. They bowed deeply and put out their tongues. But he wheeled his pony a little to one side, away from them, the American following.

"What are you afraid of?" asked the latter.

"I am not!"

"Of course you are. You're as fidgety as a cat with a tomato can tied to her tail."

"I beg your pardon?"

"Sorry, old boy—that last *simile* was rather

American. I don't imagine you do such rough things here as decorating stray felines with stray tomato cans. Besides, you've neither cats here, nor cans, nor tomatoes. But—to return to our muttons—why are you nervous? Why are you afraid? Come through, old man!"

"Spies. . . ."

"Oh——?"

"Indeed. The Dalai Lama has his agents everywhere. He does not like us to be friends with the foreigners." Kuy-go gave an involuntary little shudder. "You know the stories of this land, Rankin saheb. You know what happened to the high-priest of Gyantse when he helped those Englishmen not so many years ago?"

"Yes." The American, too, gave a little shudder. He had heard how the old high-priest, a saintly, honorable man, because he had befriended a couple of English officers who had gone over the border to shoot snow-leopards, had been called to Lhassa, had been denounced as a traitor, had been beaten, daily and publicly, for three months on the marketplace, and had then been executed. His body, denied its place amongst his predecessors, had been thrown into the river east of Lhassa, and—typically Tibetan—his soul was abolished by special decree for ever by the Grand Lama who exercises dominion not only over bodies, but even the souls of his subjects, in this as well as in the life beyond. Other instances, too, the American remembered, of savage Tibetan inhumanity against those who seem to befriend the foreigners. There had once been, for instance, a Japanese Buddhist priest, a friend of his, who had gone to Tibet on a strictly pious errand, to study the local Buddhism there; and he had just escaped with his life after entering Lhassa while three Tibetan priests who had been kind to him and had helped him with his theological studies there, had been barbarously mutilated, their hands and feet cut off, their eyes gouged out, and then left to die a lingering death in agony.

"Yes," the American repeated. "I remember."

"There you are, saheb," said Kuy-go.

"But there is the treaty!"

"The gods are stronger than the treaty!"

"But——" expostulated Rankin——"there is also the Tashi Lama's oath. The gods are surely honorable enough not to allow you to break an oath——?"

The Tibetan smiled thinly. He spoke with that typical Oriental mixture of reverence and irreverence of a nation that takes its religion as a fact, not as a theory, and is on terms of good natured familiarity with its deities.

"The gods *are* honorable," he replied. "Of

course. Or they would not be the gods. On the other hand—perhaps—are the gods also clever? Perhaps they are also shrewd? Fair warning has been given!" he repeated; and, suddenly, without another word or waiting for a reply, he whipped up his shaggy pony and galloped away up the valley, toward Phari Fort, a day's hard traveling to the north.

Rankin shook his head. He turned to Jimmie who, in the meantime, had come up and had listened intensely.

"Hear what his nibs said to me, Jimmie?" he asked.

"Yes."

"What do you make of it?"

"He is your friend. He was very sincere."

"Sure enough. I get that much. I caught the general drift. Doesn't seem to be very healthy for Monro W. Rankin in these parts, eh? But what in the name of my sainted grandaunt Priscilla did he mean by all that drivel about—oh—what was that jaw-breaking name he quoted —same that the runner from Sikhim spouted about——?"

"Srongtsan Gampo, Mr. Rankin."

"Go to the head of the class! Any idea, youngster, what it means?"

"Yes."

"All right. Spill it!"

And it was a very proud Jimmie who, out of the memories of what Ugyen Garyo and his other Tibetan friends in the Chawkpore caravanserai had told him, explained to Rankin who and what Srongtsan Gamp signified.

·CHAPTER III

NOT that Jimmie explained right then and there, in the open road, with the ice blast of the Himalayas sweeping down like a shroud of death. First they tethered and fed their hardy mules and ponies, saw that their caravan coolies found shelter with the villagers, stored their provisions beneath a triple layer of water-proofed tent cloth and, with Jimmie acting as interpreter, commenced negotiations with the head-man of Ya-tung to rent a house until they heard from the C. A. C. C. headquarters at Darjeeling.

Of course Jimmie was very interested in this, his first visit to a Tibetan town, though it was only an unimportant border place. He looked about eagerly. The streets were narrow and cluttered and exceedingly dirty, since the proper Tibetan way of cleaning house is to throw all refuse, whatever its origin or nature, out of the window into the roadway and let it remain wherever it falls. It was a lucky thing for the health of the town that the Tibetans are very fond of dogs. So numbers of them roamed through the alleys, acting as scavengers, mostly mongrels that looked like a cross between a terrier and a Chinese spaniel, and huge, mangy mastiffs.

Occasionally the monotony of the clustering, choking streets was broken by an open square. There the men of the town after their day's work—"A Paradise for Radicals," Rankin characterized it, "since nobody seems to work here more than thirty minutes every twenty-four hours"—amused themselves with various sports, wrestling, putting the stone, archery, and quoits, while in one or two tiny cafés—they seemed more like cubby holes—the same hard-working men were busy with a Tibetan variety of draughts called "Pushing the Tiger."

But, if the men refused to over-exert themselves, the women had no such objection. For they presided over a number of booths and shops that lined some of the streets, chiefly fur stores where a great variety of pelts, brought from neighboring hills by hunters and trappers, were displayed: civet-cat, weasel, lynx, otter, woolly Himalayan tiger, leopard, and also a few skins of Tibetan sable. The food stalls showed Chinese

influence. Side by side with delicious fruit, per-
simmons, mulberries, peaches, gooseberries, and
red currants, brought either south from the fertile plains about Lhassa or north from the valley
of Kashmere, were such gastronomic tit-bits as
sharks' fins all the way from the Yellow Sea, and
those ancient Pekinese eggs, black with age, which
the Tibetans imitate the Chinese in considering
an extraordinary delicacy. The more putrid and
evil-smelling they are, the greater the delicacy.
In fact they boast of them as an English country
squire boasts of his crusty old portwine, or an
American housewife of her finest, home-made
preserves or pickles.

The Afghan, a Moslem, thus clean-living,
clean-eating, turned up his intolerant nose.

"Pigs!" he commented laconically; and the
American echoed the sentiment when he had
looked into a couple of houses which were offered
him for rent.

He flatly refused when he was told that he
would have to share them with the inmates.

"Nothing doing," he said. "I'd rather sleep
out, under a puppy tent." He laughed. "I've
no race prejudice, personally, but I can't say the
same for my nose."

"I won't tell the headman your last state-
ment," smiled Jimmie, interpreting suitably, while

the Afghan mumbled into his beard that, personally, he was an honest, truth-telling man and that when he came across a grandson of pigs he liked to tell that same grandson so, and if the latter did not like it—well then—by Allah—let him eat stick—"a great deal of stick."

But Jimmie had learned enough of the gliding diplomacy of India's bazars and market-places where—to quote again the Afghan—they "choked a word until it squealed for mercy," and he interpreted so skilfully that the Tibetan never guessed the real reasons that were animating the American.

He bowed frequently and stuck his tongue out in sign of politeness and good breeding, greatly to Rankin's embarrassment and Ghula Khan's narrow-minded disgust. But he did not look directly at the newcomers; he glanced furtively, twirling his prayer wheel energetically and fingering his rosary beads to neutralize the bad, spiritual influence of dealing with foreigners, with infidels. Finally he said that there was one dwelling, uninhabited, which belonged to the Chinese *amban,* or overlord, of that part of Tibet. The *amban* was not here and used it only once in a while, when he came into the valley on occasional trips of inspection.

"Inspection?" laughed Rankin when Jimmie

had interpreted. "Graft, more likely! I know my Mongol brethren of the official classes! All right—tell him I'll take it."

"He says," replied Jimmie, "he's afraid the *amban* won't like it."

"All right—then he can lump it! Me for the house, a fire, and some breakfast! Tell him it's all right though—I'll pay for the house—and the *amban* won't kick! Why—" looking about the miserable little village—"I doubt that even a Chinaman can find much pickings here. He'll be glad enough of a few extra rupees."

The house stood a short distance away from the huddled huts made of peat sod, and seemed cleaner than the latter. For it was a rather sub- stantially built affair of cut stone and sunburnt bricks, the walls neatly white-washed, the wood- work picked out in garish colors, with charms against the Evil Eye pasted over the doorway, and from the outside it gave an air of comfort.

But as Rankin, Jimmie, and Ghula Khan en- tered, they were quickly disillusioned. The in- terior was wretched and dirty and untidy. There was little furniture; just a rudely-hewn, low bench, a bundle of malodorous Tibetan wraps as bedding, four primitive chairs, a small, gaudy shrine for the image of the household gods and, near a clay-built cook stove, a number of iron kitchen utensils strewn about; while, from pegs in the walls, were hanging provisions which the *amban* evidently kept there for his periodical visits, bladders of ancient butter—proving that the *amban* relied on the Tibetans' honesty, since butter to a large extent takes the place of money in the Forbidden Land—and skins filled with crumbly, blackish cheese, bits of dried meat, and bags of tea and flour. The chimneyless fire-hearth in the middle of the room, though presently roaring and blazing with a great fire of pine logs and dried yak dung, gave out more smell and smoke than heat.

The American laughed.

"Do you know," he asked Jimmy, "which is America's greatest lesson to the world? No? Of course democracy is all fine and dandy, and liberty, and Singer sewing machines and those flivvers that made Detroit famous. But America's most resplendent sermon—for it *is* a sermon—is—well—the good old bath tub—and don't you forget it!"

Ghula Khan's opinion was similar, though slightly more or less crude and to the point.

"When Allah created this land, He must have laughed!" he said.

But there was nothing else to do. They made the best of a bad situation, breakfasted sumptuously on things canned in far-away America and England; and it was then that Jimmie told Rankin what he knew about the mysterious Srongtsan Gampo.

It appeared that, according to Tibetan legends implicitly believed by the native peasantry, the origin of their race was truly Darwinian. For they claimed, rather with pride, that their first parent was a monkey who crossed the Himalayas and married a she-devil of the northern hills. The offspring of this interesting union was given a magical grain to eat by the Compassionate Spirit of the Mountain who, it was said, later on became the Buddha and, still later on, the Dalai Lama. But before the arrival of the first Dalai Lama, there ruled a powerful Tibetan king, Srongtsan Gampo by name, who over fifteen hundred years earlier, and a direct descendant of both the monkey and the she-devil, became endowed with the essence of the Compassionate Spirit of the Mountain, made a treaty of suzerainty with China, and married a Pekinese princess, daughter of the Yellow Emperor. It was he who built the Potala, the great palace that overtowers Lhassa, and it was his spirit—a spirit that contained within itself the essence of the Buddha, of the Compassionate Spirit of the Mountain, and of all the Dalai Lamas who have gone before—which still held sway over Tibet and whose prophecies and messages, when duly interpreted by red-capped and yellow-capped priests, were obeyed by the people to the letter.

"No doubt," drily commented the American, "that there is romance in business."

"And danger," added the Afghan. "It is hard enough to fight live foes, but foes that are dead and buried and sanctified—devils and monkeys and she-devils? Pah!" he spat. "Allah's curse on all unbelievers!"

The American laughed.

"Ghula Khan," he said, "you remind me some of my own countrymen—those rock-ribbed New England Yankees who are convinced that everybody is wrong except themselves! You aren't a Mohammedan at all, old man! At heart you're a good, old-fashioned Mayflower Puritan!"

But Ghula Khan was right when he implied that there was danger in the atmosphere. There was, of course, the Tashi Lama's oath that the lives of the C. A. C. C. agents would be safe. But, the Afghan reasoned, oath or no oath, there were also certain facts to be considered.

There was, for instance, the fact that the *Depon* had come down specially from Phari Fort to give warning.

There was, secondly, the fact of the Ya-tung villagers' behavior. During the first two or three days they were polite and kindly, and traded with the foreigners. Then a monk came down from the Lepchi monastery up the valley. He was a man evidently of low birth, with coarse, repellent features, and he stalked into their house one morning without knocking at the door.

Rankin was away at the time, attending to one of the mules that had fallen sick, and Ghula Khan, familiar with the land but only possessed of a smattering of the language, was alone with Jimmie.

"Go away," were the monk's first words, un-ceremonious, loud. "At once! Return whence you came—to India! You are not wanted here!"

"What does the unbeautiful father of seven-teen dogs want?" asked Ghula Khan.

Jimmie interpreted.

"Of course," he added, "Rankin saheb is go-ing to stay until he hears from Darjeeling."

"Naturally!" agreed the Afghan. "Tell him so!"

"I will!" replied Jimmie; but when he had told the Tibetan so the latter broke into threats.

Ghula Khan caught the spirit, if not the mean-ing of the words. He turned to Jimmie.

"I do not like his face," he said, "nor his man-ners, nor his eyes, nor his feet, nor his soul. Tell him to leave our presence. Tell him that if he refuses to, I shall cut his heart out and sell it in the bazar as an infidel butcher sells pig's tripe! Tell him anything else you feel like—but make it strong!"

And Jimmie, laughing, yet serious at heart, since, for the first time in his life he was confronted by a direct responsibility, attended to it with a sort of calm arrogance. He advanced toward the Tibetan.

"Get out of here," he said, "and stay out! Nobody invited you in!"

The Tibetan sneered. "I did not come here to bandy words—or threats, little cockroach!" he replied. "I came to give orders!"

"Whose orders?"

"The orders of Srongtsan Gampo! The orders of the Compassionate Spirit of the Mountain! The thunder gods are angry. They have spoken prophecies!"

"Have they?" Jimmie laughed. "Monk, I have lived in India all my life. I am familiar with a thousand and ten thousand gods, with a thousand and ten thousand prophecies—and," winking shamelessly at the Tibetan, "with a thousand and ten thousand monks and fakirs and priests! As to the latter—a priest in the house is like vermin in an old coat, say we of India! As to the prophecies—pah!—they are lines written on water! And as to the gods—your gods—tell them to mind their own business."

The Tibetan broke into a stream of foul abuse, but Jimmie, who had learned the art of invective in the Kashmiri bazar, outdid him. He told him in rich language exactly what he thought of him and his ancestors on both sides for seven generations back, winding up with:

"Begone, loathly beast! Back to your sty! You have pig's ears!"

The other screamed with rage. He raised his heavy, wooden prayer wheel, and was about to bring it down with full force on Jimmie's head. But the latter had had many a wicked fight in the slums of his native town. Before the Afghan had time to come to his rescue, he ducked quickly, dodged within the very curve of the monk's arm, jumped back a couple of steps then forward, launching himself like a catapult, and leaped, head foremost, like a goat, straight at the monk's comfortable stomach, at the same time bringing his feet, shod with heavy mountain-climbing boots, down on the man's toes with his whole weight. By this time the Afghan, laughing loudly, had come up, and together they rushed the monk from the room, throwing his prayer wheel after him.

"Well done, little brother!" exclaimed Ghula Khan enthusiastically. "Well done indeed, heart of my heart! I love you well! You are almost an Afghan!"

He drew Jimmie to his stout breast, compli-
menting him extravagantly, and when Rankin
returned not long afterwards, the latter congratulated him too.

"Bully for you, young fellow," he said.   "You
did exactly right!"

But the eventual results were unpleasant.

For, from that day on, the villagers of Ya-
tung ceased having dealings of any kind with
them, passed them by with averted faces, without
bowing or sticking out their tongues as politeness
demanded, and even refused to trade with them,
evidently afraid of their priestly rulers.   They
were peaceful enough, never insulted the stran-
gers nor attacked them, but there was a certain
eerie under-current of danger, here, in the chill
loneliness of the Himalayas.

Too, and chiefly, there was danger in the news
which Offan Kharo, the runner, had brought
from Darjeeling.

For, according to his report, all the three
agents of the C. A. C. C. stationed in the Chumbi
valley—one at Chalu near the Lepchi monastery,
another at Salu, and the third at Gyantse which
is the important half-way station to Lhassa—had
disappeared, at the same time.   They were Bennington, Thackeray, and Pedro de Sousa, the
first two Anglo-Indians and the other a native
born Portuguese from Goa, all three familiar

with the country and the customs, languages, and prejudices of Tibet, and all trusted employees of the C. A. C. C. who had made good at other important stations before they had been sent to the Forbidden Land. It was, the runner had reported, as 'if the hills had swallowed them. They left no message. No trace of their bodies had been found. They had simply vanished into nothingness.

Of course the C. A. C. C. people were making a thorough investigation of the affair and were keeping Rankin informed by runner almost every day as to what progress they were making. Lack of progress, rather. It was clear that— even discounting the fact that the three agents had disappeared simultaneously, as a strange co-incidence—that they had not left their stations out of their own free will. There had been no reason for it. For their books and accounts were in perfect order. Nor had they gone into the mountains to hunt and had there perished or lost their way, since all three were middle-aged men, surfeited with the thrill of killing animals. Finally, they had, as far as was known, no personal enemies and had had no trouble with the Tibetan peasants of their districts who were friendly and prosperous.

But they had disappeared. They could not be found. And Rankin shook his head.

"It's got my goat!" he mused. "Can't make it out at all. Why—there is the Tashi Lama's oath that no harm shall come to our agents!"

"There is, on the other hand, the *Depon's* warning," interrupted Ghula Khan.

"Yes!" Jimmie chimed in. "And the monk's threat—and the way the villagers behave!"

"Sure enough!" said the American. "Darned misleading and contradictory—that's what's bothering me, boys!"

It was nearly three weeks after their arrival at Ya-tung that Offan Kharo, the Sikhimese runner, came up from Darjeeling with further news —disappointing, disheartening.

"Saheb," he said, "during the last twenty days some of the cleverest detectives and trackers in India, British as well as Hindus and Tibetans in the employ of the C. A. C. C., have searched the Chumbi valley. They have questioned and cross-examined the peasants and the priests and the local Tibetan authorities——"

"Didn't the latter object to the presence of our detectives?" asked Rankin.

"Not a bit, saheb. They were friendly, gave them all the help and facilities they wanted."

"Strange!" commented the American. "It seems to prove that either the yellow-caps have nothing to do with our agents' disappearance, are perfectly innocent——"

"Or," cut in Ghula Khan, "that they are as guilty as Shaitan himself, but are quite sure that their guilt can never be found out."

Offan Kharo inclined his head.

"Yes," he said. "And our detectives have found out nothing—have proved nothing."

"Not even a suspicion?"

"No, saheb?"

"What's to be done?" asked Rankin.

"The C. A. C. C. has asked the British-Indian government to take up the case with the Dalai Lama, through diplomatic channels——"

"Hm—" the American shrugged his shoulders, "official red-tape—I know—takes a year to wind it up, and another year to unwind it—and by the time the Indian government is ready to talk turkey to the yellow-caps, our agents, if they are still alive, will have disappeared for good, and all the business of the C. A. C. C. will have gone up in smoke."

"But what else can be done, saheb?" countered the runner. "Headquarters advises you to return to India."

"Eh?" Rankin looked up sharply, angrily. "Return—you said?"

"Yes, saheb."

"Not if I know it!"

"But——"

"I shan't quit under fire!"

Rankin hit the table with his clenched fist.

"Danger be blowed!" he exclaimed. "I'm used to danger. I've lived in Chicago and dodged flivvers! No—" he was serious again— "we're not going to let this beast of a land get the best of us and kick us out via the back door without a darned good scrap, are we, boys?" turning to Jimmie and Ghula Khan. "Are you with me?"

"Yes!" replied the two, in unison; and the American laughed.

"The Three Musketeers!" he exclaimed. "Modern, Asiatic edition! A Californian, an Afghan, and—what exactly are *you*, Jimmie?"

"James Clinton Weatherby, American and gentleman!" came the stout reply.

"Sure enough!" smiled Rankin. He turned to the runner. "Go back to headquarters and tell them we're going to stick it out until we've found the three agents."

Then, when Offan Kharo had gone off again on the long trek south across the border, he told Jimmie and Ghula Khan about his plans.

"I assume," he said, "that the Tibetan authorities are guilty. But it's up to us to prove it. I don't think that our lives are exactly in danger and that the Tashi Lama will break his oath, in spite of all the warnings and threats and prophecies. But we have our work cut out. You,

Ghula Khan, know the country hereabouts, and you, Jimmie, the language. I know darned little except business and how to boss an outfit. Very well. The first C. A. C. C. station is at Chalu—that's where old Tom Bennington used to be before they caused him to vanish into thin air. It's a day's trip to Chalu via the regular route, through the Chumbi. And we can't afford to take that route—can't afford to let the whole Forbidden Land know what we are doing. So early tomorrow morning you two better sneak out of here—take along rifles as if you were going hunting—and see if you can't locate another trail, not quite so frequented and obvious as the Chumbi. In the meantime I'll pay off the coolies and send them back to India with most of our supplies. For we'll have to travel light and sudden, I guess."

So, very early the next morning, while the villagers of Ya-tung were still asleep, Jimmie and the Afghan struck out northwest from Ya-tung, across the hills, leaving the Chumbi valley to one side.

It was icy cold, forty degrees below zero, with a terrific gale that swept down from the upper land and the far glaciers of Chumelhari in the north, and they had to dig their short, stout alpenstocks into the frozen, slippery ground at every step. Here and there the wind had swept the snow from the steep mountainsides, and the coloring had a weird, unnatural look: bare, rocky hills, of a glowing ochre, streaked with dull reds and purples and greens, and barred with bands of yellow sandstone and the silvery grey and black of basalt.

The Afghan grumbled most of the time, at himself, at Fate, but chiefly at the country and its inhabitants.

"Allah!" he cried. "Why did I ever leave my own land? The saying is true: when greed enters, wisdom withdraws. Decidedly, if I ever should return to my own country—which I doubt —I shall never leave it again, but live an upright and decent life, virtuous and charitable and kind to everybody—even to unbelievers!"

"Oh yes!" laughed Jimmie. "I know! The cat ate nine hundred chickens—and then went on pilgrimage!"

The road grew steadily worse. Masses of fog-clouds rolled overhead, blurring the outlines of the mountains. When these fogs lifted, curling themselves up in the strong wind like a grey curtain of smoke, or dissolved in thin snow showers, they disclosed the scanty, scraggly trees and the jagged rocks covered with a glassy coating of ice-crystals from their freezing vapors, making the trail as slippery as a snake.

They were blue and benumbed, their breath

whistling painfully through tortured lungs, their ears roaring with the tremendous blood pressure, when at last the sun came out with a bit of thawing warmth and gold. But Ghula Khan, a born mountaineer and as sure-footed as a mule, leading and lending a helping hand, they made fair progress, cut sharply away from the winding Chumbi valley, and shortly before noon partly by luck, partly—perhaps chiefly—due to the Afghan's unerring, hill-bred instinct of direction, they found a narrow rock trail that zigzagged through the welter of peaks and crags and presently broadened into what seemed a disused road. For as the rocks receded to both sides, giving place to a mountain pasture where wild yaks and golden-colored Tibetan wild-asses, were nibbling at the scanty grass beneath the snow blanket, they passed a number of dilapidated, sacred cairns, some ruined water-mills for grinding corn, and occasionally a crumbling, square pillar of masonry faced by carved stones that bore the mystic legend of the Dalai Lama: *Om ma-ni pad-me! Hung!*, each syllable painted in a different color—all sure indications that once a settlement had been there.

Farther up the road they saw a Tibetan peasant who was driving a herd of yaks to the west.

"Drop behind a rock!" whispered Jimmie to

the Afghan, for while he himself, dressed as he was, his head swathed in a woolen scarf so that little of the face was visible, and in perfect command over the language, could pass easily enough for a native of one of the border states, the Afghan would be immediately recognized as a foreigner, since he spoke little Tibetan and—orthodox, old-fashioned, narrow-minded Moslim that he was—had refused to shave off his beard.

"Right!" said Ghula Khan, dropping on the ground behind a huge stone before the peasant had seen him; and Jimmie walked up to the latter, bowing politely and sticking out his tongue, the other showing his good-nature and good-breeding by similar amenities.

Jimmie, representing himself to be a Bhotanese in the employ of the *Depon,* told the Tibetan that he had lost his way, that he was trying to reach Chalu, but had wandered away from the road on the trail of some game, and—he asked—could he reach Chalu by following the road he was on now?

"Go back to the Chumbi valley," advised the Tibetan, pointing east—"over there!"

"But can't I keep on this road?"

"Yes and no," replied the unsuspecting peasant, explaining that once the road had been in good order but that several years ago, a few miles south of Chalu, a mountain slide had blocked the way, that it was hard for even an expert mountaineer to overcome the obstacle, and that in consequence the small settlements hereabouts had been abandoned since they had no market nearer than Chalu for their produce.

Jimmie thanked the man; then, when the latter had disappeared around a bend, he called to the Afghan who rose, and told him what he had found out.

"What do you think, Ghula Khan?" he wound up.

"We know the road is right. It goes to Chalu."

"Yes. But what about the mountain slide?"

The other shrugged his massive shoulders. "We'll try it if Rankin saheb gives the word. Let's return."

It was late in the evening when they reached Ya-tung. As they entered the valley where the little settlement was huddled they found that heavy snow had fallen during the day, clothing everything in a thick garb of white.

"Back again, Rankin saheb!" shouted the Afghan as they opened the door.

But there was no answer, except the eerie, hollow, mocking echo brushing down from the rafters; and it was only then that it struck them as strange that there had been no light shining behind the windows of stiff, oiled paper.

"Rankin saheb!" called Jimmie, prey to a terrible foreboding of disaster. "Why—" he slurred, stopped.

They rushed across the threshold, lit the lamps filled with yak-fat, and looked about them.

The room was silent, empty.

They looked at each other. They were afraid even to think.

"Do you believe that—?" began Ghula Khan.

"Perhaps—" stammered Jimmie—"he has gone into the village, to talk to the people, or to our coolies?"

"Perhaps!"

But when they went to the village they found that the coolies, doubtless obeying Rankin's orders, had left early that morning for India, taking most of the supplies along, while the villagers shrugged their shoulders. Nobody had seen the American, they declared, averting their faces and twirling their prayer-wheels. Nobody had spoken to him. And the answer remained the same, though Jimmie cajoled and begged, though the Afghan stormed and bullied and threatened physical violence.

"Gone!" said Jimmie as they returned to their house, "gone like——"

"Like the others—the agents of the C. A.

C. C.!"   The Afghan spat.   "Allah's curse on all unbelievers!"

"What now?" asked Jimmie.

"Hayah!   What now?" echoed the Afghan dully.

CHAPTER IV

"THERE are two things we can do," said Jimmie the next morning. "We can carry on, we two alone, here in the hills until we have found Mr. Rankin, or we can return to Darjeeling and report to the C. A. C. C. and ask for orders."

"You talk," smiled Ghula Khan, "as if you were already a trusted servant of the C. A. C. C."

"I am going to be—some day," came the steady reply. "Shall we go, or stay?"

"What do you think yourself?"

"I want to stay," said Jimmie, "and find Mr. Rankin. I like him. And once he saved me— he paid my fine when the magistrate imprisoned me unjustly."

"I like him, too," the Afghan smiled thinly— "though my reason for not returning to India is not altogether one of unselfish affection for the saheb." And then, in a burst of confidence, typical of his race which is secretive, suspicious, then, suddenly, without logical reason, trusts implicitly, he told Jimmie why he had left India, why he had enrolled himself in Rankin's service, crossing with him into Tibet, away from the jurisdiction of the British Raj.

"My name was not always Ghula Khan," he began, "nor was I always so orthodox a Moslim as to insist on wearing a beard. Once—" he glanced obliquely at the other—"I was known as Shahgassi Aman Popiljai——"

"Shahgassi—?" asked Jimmie, excited, thrilled, remembering the gliding gossip of the Kashmiri bazar, "you mean—the raider, the gun-runner?"

"The same!" the other replied, not without pride. "In those days men, including the British, feared me and women did not altogether dislike me. My face," he added naively, "was very handsome. So I went clean-shaven that people could see and admire. Now—" he laughed— "I wear a beard. It is the best disguise in the world."

Jimmie listened. He was delighted, interested, and a little awed. Shahgassi Aman Popiljai! The Jesse James and Captain Kidd and Henry Hawkins and Sitting Bull rolled into one of Indian boys' envy and imagination! He stared at the man. He remembered how often, in the past, he and his pals had played at Shahgassi Aman Popiljai and his enemies, making the bazars ring with the noise and riot of their game. He remembered, too, how they had decided to emulate the example of the notorious borderer. And here was the latter, in the flesh, smiling upon him with a flash of white, even teeth. And, these past weeks, he had bandied words with him; had been congratulated by him because of his pluck, had become his friend. At the thought, Jimmie felt elated and proud. He hardly believed his good luck.

"So you are really Shahgassi?" he asked. "Really?"

"Yes."

"But—" asked Jimmie—"what happened? Why are you now Ghula Khan—a mountain guide—and in Tibet?"

"Because," smiled the Afghan, "I would rather hear people say of me: 'He fled! Disgrace upon him!' than: 'He was slain! Allah have mercy upon him!' Because, in other words, I respect the safety of my own skin—unbeautiful though it be—just a trifle less than I respect the Blessed Messenger Mohammed—Peace on Him and His Family!"

"Please tell me," begged Jimmie; and the other did.

For years Shahgassi Aman Popiljai had harassed the border, the leader of a handful of wild Pathans and Afghans. The British had never been able to catch him, though they sent against him horse, foot and guns. He was as evasive as the morning mist. He was here today and there tomorrow, taking toll in gold and cattle, sending the flames licking across the villages, dancing out of the hills and the jungles with his savage followers, looting, burning, striking swiftly and mercilessly and always at the very place where he was not supposed to be. Many punitive expeditions were sent, but they had no results except footsore native soldiers and white officers down with fever and cursing their luck. At last the British, being a sensible race, always ready to compromise, made a treaty with him, forgave him his many iniquities, and—like a great statesman, weary with brilliant and honorable service for the State—pensioned him off. He retired on a country estate near Peshawur. Two years he lived there. Then the lack of excitement began to irk him, and he looked about him to see what he might do to vary the monotony of his peaceful existence.

Now, not very far from Peshawur, on a neutral strip of first-class mountain scenery between the Afghan province of Kabulistan and the British-Indian Northwest Frontier province, lived some hooknosed, ruffianly, bushy-bearded gentlemen who called themselves the tribe of Ahmet-Khel and claimed to be extremely good Moslims, easily led into *jehad*, into holy war—as long as the prospects of loot rose flush with the prospects of spiritual gains.   Often they looked down from their mountains eerie into the broad, smiling plains of Hindustan, and envied.   But past experiences had taught them that it was impossible to fight with Khaibar knives and muzzle-loaders against machine guns and magazine rifles. Therefore it became their ambition to purchase several thousand of the latter variety, including many rounds of ammunition.   Therefore, too, the British proclaimed a law which made it high treason, punishable by death, to do "gun-running," to sell as much as a single rifle to the people beyond the border, and had instructed the secret service to see to the detection of the crime and the enforcement of the law.

In consequence the price of rifles beyond the border rose higher and higher until even a light fowling-piece brought its weight in silver, and until Ghula Khan—then still known as Shahgassi Aman Popiljai—saw not only the excitement that might be had but also the handsome profit a shrewd and daring middleman could realize out of a few caravan loads of rifles and bullets.

He communicated with the headmen of the Ahmet-Khel; also with a number of unscrupulous as well as unclassified people in Calcutta, Amritsar, Bombay, Aden—here and there and everywhere.   And a bargain was struck.   The guns and bullets were purchased in Chicago through a Hamburg house that used an Argentine agent and shipped the stuff in a Norwegian tramp from Charleston, S. C., to India in a roundabout way, via Honolulu, New Zealand, and Vladivostok. It reached a certain town in India's Bikaner desert by dribbles, was packed into camel loads marked peacefully "Salt," "Machinery," and "Canned Goods," and passed under the nose of the British authorities via Peshawur, through the Khaibar pass, into the northwestern foothills.

Shahgassi Aman Popiljai—known later on as Ghula Khan—commanded the caravan, ostensibly on a friendly visit to his home village.

Then came a little pebble which stopped the wheels of his chariot of progress.

For a pack-horse reared and squealed.   An Afghan driver cursed and spat and brought down the point of his dagger.   The horse reared more than ever, rolled into the snow, and burst the rope which held its load.

The load struck a rock.

And just then Shafizullah Yar, Punjaubi, known to the Indian secret service as C 22, and Nath Chundrajee, his Bengali comrade known as C 79, dropped from a mountain crest, looked at the contents of the bundle—and asked Shahgassi Aman Popiljai the Why and How and Whence and Whereto?"

"And so," Ghula Khan wound up the tale, "I, being a quick-thinking man, recommended their souls into the keeping of Allah, the One, the All-Merciful, and fired from the hip—twice.   And those two dogs crimsoned the snow with their life's blood, while—seeing British soldiers here and there amongst the rocks, scrambling down, some shooting—I went away from there very quickly.   And I went into retirement and let my beard grow, and now I am no longer Shahgassi Aman Popiljai, but Ghula Khan, and—ahee!— most decidedly shall I refuse to return to India! They have spies out after me, and the Raj's laws are harsh, and I have only one life—which I love dearly."

Jimmie laughed.

"What do you think we had better do?" he asked.

"It was Rankin saheb's plan to go to Chalu, to look for traces of Bennington saheb. Let us start this afternoon. We know the other route. If we find the first saheb who disappeared, we shall also doubtless find the others, including Rankin. We must travel swift and light. It will be a difficult journey. For the winter is hard, and there is the mountain slide."

They spent the morning talking over their plans and packing the minimum of necessities they could take along, and a little before noon they were ready to start when the door opened and in came the monk who, a few weeks earlier, had ordered them to leave and had been thrown out by the combined efforts of Jimmie and Ghula Khan.

"Tell your friend," were his first words to Jimmie, "that resistance is useless. Tell him in his own language that it would be wise for him to throw up his hands!" And a moment later he stepped fully inside, followed by a dozen Tibetan soldiers, their regimental insignia embroidered in scarlet and black on their rough felt tunics, their rifles leveled with businesslike precision.

Jimmie was thunderstruck. He looked at the Afghan, translating rapidly. The latter asked Jimmie to find out what it was all about and to remind the monk—"that unclean descendant of

a thousand first-class she-devils!" he called him—
that there was a treaty between the Dalai Lam
and the British Raj.

Jimmie interpreted and the monk smiled.

"I know that there is a treaty," he said, "a
treaty of peace and amity and good-will!   And
can there be a better proof of our good-will and
friendship for the British than to return to them,
warned by the Raj's spies, one Ghula Khan, formerly known as Shahgassi Aman Popiljai—"
the Afghan looked up quickly as he heard the familiar name—"a gun-runner and assassin?"

He laughed, gave a guttural cry of command,
and three of the soldiers cleared the room.

"Let us fight them, O Afghan!" cried Jimmie.
"I shall help you!"

He suited the deed to the words, hurling himself against one of the attackers.   It was lucky
for both him and Ghula Khan that the room was
small and that by this time the soldiers had distributed themselves about the place so that they
could not fire their rifles without endangering
each other.   Yet, try as he might, Jimmie's struggle was short.   Two of the men, huge, broad,
hulking mountaineers, set upon him, and in no
time at all had him backed into a corner where
they proceeded to truss him up with a rope.   So
he was there, helpless, furious, watching the
homeric battle which his friend was putting up,

even, as he was struggling, throwing a laughing word to Jimmie that he knew how great were the odds against him, that he had neither chance nor hope of winning, but that he would like to "maul these ill-smelling descendants of ten thousand first-class devils a bit before they pulled him down!"

So he fought, employing tactics and obtaining results that would cause an American lumber jack or stevedore to turn green with impotent envy. He dodged, danced, gouged, grappled, kicked, bit, and scratched. He used fists and feet and head. His breath came in short, staccato bursts. At one and the same time he was trying to land blow, to parry blow, to sidestep kicking legs and crashing elbows. He did not have his dagger in his waist shawl, and had to rely on nature's weapons.

A rough knuckle caught him on the left temple, an open palm hit the point of his chin; one of the soldiers, dodging within the very crook of Ghula Khan's powerful right arm, grappled close while several others closed in the next moment like hounds pulling down a stag.

Ghula Khan felt himself seized about the chest under the armpits by a bearlike grasp. For a second he felt as if his ribs were crushing in his lungs. His temples throbbed, the roof of his mouth felt parched.

Straining, cursing, he fell to the ground, one of the Tibetans on top of him, another booting him in the ribs, a third dancing about, watching his chance for a knockout blow. Then, with a sudden hard bunching of muscles, Ghula Khan pinioned his first assailant's arms to his sides, spread his strong legs, and, with a great jerk and heave, freed himself.

It was at this moment that Jimmie noticed a short dagger that had dropped on the floor from the waist shawl of one of the Tibetans.

He could reach it with his foot.

"Ghula Khan! Hey—Ghula Khan!" he called out, and when the other turned his head, he kicked the dagger towards him.

The Afghan picked it up, and went to the attack.

He used the dagger like a rapier, with carte and tierce, with lunge and thrust and counter-thrust and quick, staccato ripost, pinking here a leg, there a grimy hand, and ripping through tough felt coats as with the edge of a razor.

In and at them with a stamping of feet, a harsh, guttural war yell.

Jimmie felt like applauding. He forgot all about the seriousness of the situation. He simply enjoyed the savage, picturesque spectacle.

Then, all at once, he gave a cry of warning. Just a little too late. For the monk had crept up behind Ghula Khan, brought his heavy wooden prayer wheel down upon the other's head, and knocked him down.

Immediately, before he could jump to his feet, one of the soldiers had used the opportunity, had bent down and, quickly, skilfully, snapped rusty Chinese hand-cuffs about the Afghan's wrists.

They pulled him up, led him away. Ghula Khan shrugged his shoulders, offering no more resistance. He turned on the threshold and called over to Jimmie.

"Allah alone is great!" he said. "Who am I to fight against Allah's will, the which is fate—fate which is bound around the necks of all of us, rich and poor, prince or peasant—fate that comes out of the dark and strikes, like a blind camel, without warning or jingling of bells? But tell me, little brother—did you not once boast that, although a flea, you can bite? Very well! Jump—leap like a flea—bite—and free Rankin saheb! I shall endeavor to fool these Tibetan dogs and escape and join you. If I fail—*wah!* —fate is fate! Allah's blessing on you, little brother!"

They dragged him out, while the monk remained. He walked over to Jimmie and cut the ropes that bound him. Then he sat down and smiled blandly, benignly.

"I bear you no ill-will," he said presently, "be-cause of—ah—the little disagreement that hap-pened a few weeks ago. I am To Palté, a yellow-cap from the Lepchi monastery. I am a devout believer in the excellent Buddha's princi-ples of forgiveness. No. I bear you no ill-will. On the contrary—I shall reward bad deeds with good. I shall give you most unselfish advise."

Jimmie did not reply. It seemed to him as if, suddenly, his childhood, his youth, had dropped away from him like a useless garment. And—there were his father's last words—he vaguely remembered them—something about thinking, thinking well, then acting at once.

He heard again the monk's words:

"You are now quite alone!"

"Quite alone!" agreed Jimmie, warily, watch-ing the other from beneath lowered eyelids, thinking furiously the while, wondering what he should do.

"And you are young, and in a strange land!" went on To Palté, passionlessly.

"Indeed!"

"My advice is for you to go away. Go back to India. It would be wise—and healthy. What do you think?"

Doubtless the monk was right, considered Jimmie.   He *was* alone, and young, and in a strange land.   And yet—there was Rankin saheb, his friend, who had helped him; there was his racial pride which commanded him to carry on; there was, dimly, in his mind a national American message.

He looked up.

"Perhaps you are right," he said.   "I shall let you know."

"When?"

"This afternoon.   Just before sun-down. Then I shall tell you my decision."

"I trust it will be a wise decision," said the monk.

"So do I!"

"*Om ma-ni pad-me! Hung!*" mumbled To Palté piously, and he left the house, energetically twirling his prayer wheel, while Jimmie looked after him, a prey to conflicting emotions, but resolved in his mind as to his duty.

Only one thing mattered, he told himself. Rankin, his friend, who had helped him when he was in trouble.   Very well.   He would pay—in full.

Of course he was afraid.   He was, in fact, too plucky not to be afraid.   But he acted.   Rapidly, as soon as he had watched the monk disappear around a jutting rock which marked the place where the village, properly speaking, lay huddled, he re-packed his supplies, adding the Afghan's to his own, as well as certain of Rankin's, chiefly—for he might have to travel at night, he considered—an electric flashlight. The pack, he thought, was not too heavy. Then he picked up Ghula Khan's dagger, slipped it into his waist-shawl, looked his rifle over, oiled and loaded it, and, on second consideration, since he could not take it along, broke the lock of Ghula Khan's rifle. Then he put on his heavy outer clothes, stepped to the door, and looked out.

The snow had again begun to fall in big, blinding whirls, hiding the village of Ya-tung. Warily he watched for a few minutes. There was no sign of life. So he left the house and stepped out at a good pace, the snow obliterating his tracks as fast as he put down his feet. Carefully, doubling up his body here and there behind rock or snow-drift or gnarled tree, he left the confines of Ya-tung, and took the route to the northwest which he and the Afghan had used the morning before.

He was off toward Chalu; off to match his wits and courage against those of the Forbidden Land.

And he felt very young, and very much alone.

CHAPTER IV

HALF an hour later the blizzard stopped suddenly, cut off as clean as with a knife, and
Jimmie made good headway. More and more,
as if by hereditary memory, was he becoming used
to the cold. A little after sun-down he reached
the disused road where he had met and questioned the Tibetan peasant the day before, and
he slept that night in one of the dilapidated
water-mills. He was off early the following
morning, after swallowing a hasty breakfast.
Again there was no snow, and the dry air was
filled with a biting, killing frost. Nature itself
seemed as if benumbed beneath the blighting hand
of winter. No hum of insect was heard, nor the
sound of beast or bird except, presently, as the
road crossed a forest of pines and junipers with
needles that winter had transformed into sprays

of diamond-crystals, an occasional red-start, a few pert, scarlet-legged choughs and pale-feathered snow-pigeons, and once an eagle soaring high on stiffly extended pinions. Twice he crossed steep-banked streams on thin, hard ribbons of ice that streaked from rock to rock; he crossed with perfect safety, though he could hear the gurgle of water burrowing its way underneath.

Once more, in the afternoon, the snow fell thick, and now Jimmie welcomed it. For his feet were growing tired, the road had become very rocky, and the snow improved it by clogging the dangerous spaces between jagged, sharp-cornered stones and building here and there a white causeway across a frozen, slippery river-slide.

Again that night he found a ruined house where he slept, and was off again early, suffering now from the cold which had dropped to fifty degrees below zero. Too, an icy wind blew, peeling the exposed parts of his face with a pelting hurricane of grit, gravel, broken icicles, and small pebbles, and forcing him to a distinct mental and physical effort every time he breathed the air through his pumping, hurting lungs, so he was glad when, shortly after the noon hour, the road dipped deep into a saucer-like depression, where it was warmer, thanks both to the lower altitude and the presence of some hot springs.

He had taken some provisions along, carefully chosen so as to weigh as little as possible, consisting mostly of dried yak-meat and Tibetan bread, made of parched barley meal and kneaded with water into a doughy, tasteless paste, then baked over an open, smelly yak-dung fire—not very appetizing, but nourishing enough judging from the physique of the Tibetan hillmen who, for months at a time, lived on nothing else. He had also brought a package of salt and some of Mr. Rankin's American patent matches in case he should be able to find and kill game or birds. He found a chance an hour later when he startled a woolly snow hare and brought it down with a shot and, not long afterwards, when he killed a wild goose on the wing. He broiled the meat, ate heartily, drank some of the snow water, and resumed his march.

Once he lost his way, and from the edge of a precipice had a sight of a genial valley where the peasants were at work, busy with the new season's crops. But, not wishing to be seen, he turned quickly, passing through a small sequestered glen where flocks of sand-grouse sped swiftly past him, and where a few Brahmany ducks whirred noisily among the reedy hummocks that fringed a little river's limpid, turquoise depths.

Again he passed into the higher hills through

a rocky cleft and down what seemed the moraine of a former glacier.   An hour later he found the trail once more.

He was getting tired; he tripped and tumbled like a boat in a short sea, and the rifle rubbed his shoulder raw while the knapsack filled with supplies grew heavier with every step.   But he kept on, not only because of the duty which he had marked out for himself, but also because—and it had come suddenly—a peculiar fear had swept down upon him this last half hour or so.   He tried to explain it away, to reason it out of existence by telling himself that he was wearied and nervous and over-fatigued, but the fact of this fear remained: it was as if some unseen, yet terrible presence were following him, hounding his foot-steps, and frequently he glanced over his shoulder.   He stopped, shuddered, gave a little choked cry as he imagined that a blotched, grey shadow was behind him, an elusive shadow, without a body, which had joined him unbidden. Even as he watched, it disappeared, it seemed to float up the side of the nearest rock and melt into the dead-white of the sky.   Then he gave a relieved laugh—it had only been the shadow of a low-flung cloud driven before the wind.

But his fear remained, his nervousness, his uneasy expectancy of something which his common sense refused to believe or formulate.   Ever and again he imagined that a gliding, bodiless shadow was leaping after him from rock to rock, and once he could have sworn that he heard a harsh, jeering laugh shattering the stillness.

He called himself a fool in English and Hindu, clenched his teeth, and kept on.

The disused road lay now in a north-northeasterly direction, flanked by low, hog-backed hills of red sandstone and bright porphry without any indication of snow and here and there a bit of plant life, trailing length of wood-briar, some hardy grasses, and a clump of rhodo-dendron scrub. Half an hour later he came through a basalt field, treading his way slowly, painfully, on bruised and bleeding feet across the rugged blocks. It was a typical Bad Lands, a desert peopled only with echoes, a place of death for what little there was in it to die—a wilder-ness. He made camp and rested near an enor-mous, gnarled throne-tree. He looked about him.

To the west stretched a huge, grey flat, with long lines of basalt seaming the surface and with wide sheets of tufaceous gypsum which glittered like mirrors in the sun. Straight ahead of him something like a stony, jagged buttress tilted up to the sky, crest rising above crest, crag above crag, into the far sky, and Jimmie told himself that this was the mountainslide, the mighty landslip which, according to the Tibetan peasant, was blocking the road.

Chalu was on the other side of it, a day's journey from Ya-tung via the direct route of the Chumbi valley. He had been two days on the march, and here was still the greatest obstacle to overcome. And how was he going to do it, he, born and bred in the plains?

"Hard even for an expert mountaineer!" the Tibetan had told him.

"Got to try it just the same!" he said to himself, and rose.

As he neared it, he saw that the landslip which barred the way was acting like a gigantic dam, over two thousand feet high, across which a river tumbled drunkenly in a series of foaming cascades, forming at the base half a dozen great pools silted up by the mud and alluvial slime deposited by the torrents. Wild ducks were swimming there and wading and preening their garish plumage while, farther to the east, on a grassy meadow spangled with the delicate tracery of the frost, he saw a number of blood-pheasants and tragopans.

There were still, here and there, the remains of former settlements. They were quite uninhabitable. There was neither house nor hut, just a mass of wind-bleached fragments of stucco reliefs, probably the relics of some ancient

burial-place or perhaps a Buddhist temple. Still
keeping on his way, he came upon a bit of land
where he could trace the ground plan of what
must once have been a substantial building,
marked by the remains of walls fashioned of
plastered reed-matting. Too, he could trace the
positions once occupied by large pottery jars for
storing butter sunk into the mud floor and of similar appurtenances of Tibetan house-keeping.
Presently he came upon more walls and broken
bits of pottery, but all was petrified, eroded away
by wind and winter and cold. There were, too,
the ruins of what must once have been a Buddhist
monastery, lording it over the settlement in
priestly arrogance. For he saw still, painted on
tumbled walls, countless repetitions of the Grand
Lama's spell, the *"Om ma-ni pad-me! Hung!—*
Hail, Jewel in the Lotus Flower!"*, that universal
panacea for all Tibetan spiritual and bodily ills;
saw painted on a tool-fashioned rock a faded
painting of the Buddhist Lady of Mercy, a sort
of local Virgin Mary who is the especial patron
saint of those who are in distress upon the mountains as well as of sailors on the sea; saw fallen
stone tablets bearing pious texts and sentences in
ornamented Tibetan letters; saw a vista of
broken, pillared nave and aisles and a small chapel
with the remains of a high altar on which once
the great, golden butter lamps had burnt their

sacred fires before the gilt, turquoise-studded images.

There was even, farther on, one of those flattened tall rocks, carved with grisly, ceremonial bas-relief figures, from which the dead bodies are thrown to be devoured by dogs, vultures, crows, and other carrion feeders. For this is the Tibetan method of disposing of their dead— doubtless due in part to the difficulty of digging the frozen soil for graves.

Jimmie walked on. Suddenly he stumbled over something. Instinctively he bent down and looked, and instantly gave an exclamation of surprise.

"Why—what——?"

He picked it up; examined it.

It was the red clay bowl of a Tibetan pipe, recently used, he could tell, by the ashes still sticking to the inside. He sniffed it. There was no doubt. He could smell the acrid tobacco with the faint aroma of opium.

He stood still; endeavored to puzzle out the mystery contained in that bit of red clay, found there, in the heart of the stony Tibetan wilderness.

Perhaps, he thought, some nomad shepherd may have passed through here with his animals. For there were the grass meadows at the foot of the landslip. But, try as he might, he could find no trace of animals, yaks or sheep or ponies, having passed that way. The grass was untrampled. Farther on, the rock dust lay in an even, untouched coating. Furthermore, he asked himself, where could the shepherd have come from? East and west towered ranges of hills which barred the way, empty of vegetation, not the sort of ground to attract a pastoral nomad. North the mountain slide, beyond the pools, stood like a wall. Nor, finally, had there been trace of man or beast the way he had come, from the south and southwest.

Who then had smoked the pipe? And when?

He remembered his nervous imaginings that somebody had dodged his footsteps, that a bodiless shadow had followed him, gliding batlike from boulder to boulder. But—no!—this pipe bowl he had found in front of him, the way he was going, could not have been dropped by anybody who had come after. On the other hand, since the bowl had recently been used, and since there was no trail east or west which anybody might have used, the smoker must have come from the direction straight ahead, north, from the mountain slide, must then have turned and gone back the way he had come.

He looked at the mountain slide, as if for an answer to the questions and fear in his mind. Then the idea came to him that nobody, not even the most expert mountaineer, after climbing up or down this sheer precipice, would have enough wind or energy left to smoke a pipe.   Therefore, was his next thought, there must be a way through the landslip by which it could be more easily traversed, perhaps a tunnel——

He studied the great, rocky obstacle with his sharp, blue eyes.   He was still on the farther side of the pools formed by the tumbling mountain torrent, but he noticed presently that, across one of them, a sort of ford was marked by half-submerged stones.   He crossed to the other side.

Here the gigantic landslip reared directly above him, steep and forbidding, most of the mass of granite which composed it bare and wind-swept, but some of the boulders clad with a sparse growth of yellow gorse bushes and bright-pink pedicularis.   By this time Jimmie had become enough of a hillman to realize that wherever there is gorse in the mountains there is also sand for it to grow in, and that wherever there is sand among steep rocks there must be a bit of level ground and therefore a place to put one's feet.   So, carefully balancing his weight, he reached up with his right hand and then took hold of a tough gorse bush while, his body stiffly aslant as he had seen Ghula Khan do many a time, he inserted the alpenstock into a stone fissure with his left hand, using it as a brake.

After an attempt or two he succeeded. He drew himself up, overcame his dizziness with an effort, and found that he was on an extremely narrow ledge that led west, swinging out of sight around a bend.

Walking carefully and slowly, squeezing his body tight against the rocky face of the landslip, and handling the alpenstock sideways like a rudder, he moved along this ledge, and he noticed with a thrill of excitement that the sand which covered it bore the faint imprint of footsteps. He said to himself that he would follow the footsteps wherever they led, and so he kept on until, just after he had turned to bend, he saw that the ledge came sharply to an end. For he found himself directly in front of a great, flat stone set into the living rock like a door. It was smooth and even, evidently tool-cut, and painted, each syllable in a different color, with the mystic legend of the Dalai Lama: *"Om ma-ni pad me! Hung!* Hail, Jewel in the Lotus Flower."

"Think!" said Jimmie to himself. "Think well—then act—at once!"

He thought that, since the footsteps stopped here and since the threatening, sheer granite wall above gave no hold or support, even to a wildgoat, they must have passed through. So he acted. He looked for a lever, a handle, a knob, a hidden contrivance, anything to open the slab,

found none.   In plain weariness he finally leaned
against the slab, pressing down on the alpenstock
to preserve his balance on the narrow ledge, and
he felt as if something was giving way behind
him.   Quickly he squirmed, turned—there was
not so very much room—and he saw that the
stone had moved a little.   So he pressed against
it with all his force, and it slid with a half turn,
evidently revolving on a pivot.

He stopped, looked; saw before him what
seemed to be a grotto or a cave; nature-made or
man-made, or perhaps, he thought, a combined
result of both nature and man, the former at the
time of the mountain slide having heaped a stony
envelope around some of the buildings when the
great avalanche swept across the valley.

He stepped over the threshold into semi-
darkness, and felt steps under his feet.   Slowly,
carefully, he groped his way down a number of
steps, worn slippery and hollow.

He snapped on the button of his electric torch,
sending a sharp ray of light ahead of him, and he
found that there were several caves communicating with each other; saw too, that their walls
were decorated with mural paintings in ancient,
cracked and grangrened tempora.   Familiar
since his childhood with Asia and Asia's many
faiths and many divinities, he saw that the paintings were very old and conventionalized, giving

scenes from the Buddhist scriptures showing the
Lord Gautama enthroned among the minor
Buddhas and disciples, the Bodhisattvas, who
were standing on lotus leaves and praying.

He was in a peculiar state of mind. His feet
followed through the caves. But his mind
seemed detached from his bodily organs. Somehow, he felt that he had stepped into a hollow—
not a hollow of the earth, but one of time; a hollow of the night which the centuries had over-
looked, and where the unknown powers and mys-
teries of the Forbidden Land were holding him
and sucking him in deeper and deeper in the
stretch of their gigantic, changeless hands. He
felt a prey to enormous, voiceless excitement.

But he walked on, until he came to a larger
cave.

Here, too, the walls were painted with typical
scenes of Buddhist legends. On the left was
Lord Gautama standing, dressed in a simple robe
of that dark, red-brown color which Indian tra-
dition since ancient times prescribes for ascetics
and saintly teachers of all sects.

Jimmie was about to pass on, when something
in the painting struck him as peculiar. He had
always taken a great interest in the Forbidden
Land, its peoples and customs and faiths and
superstitions. He had listened by the hour to
the duffel-clad hillmen in the Chawkpore caravan-

serai, had looked at the curious, highly colored prayer flags, decorated with Tibetan legends, in bazars, until he had become as familiar with tales from the Buddha's life as a young American with anecdotes from the life of Benjamin Franklin, and until he had seen as many paintings of the Buddha as the American boy sees of "Washington Crossing the Delaware."

Now he noticed that, in the painting in front of him, while the Buddha's right hand was raised in the correct, traditional pose, known as that of Abhaya or Protection, the left, which should have been hanging flat against the side, was lifted in a pointing gesture.

Instinctively his eyes followed the direction in which the hand was extended.

He looked.

There was a small opening in the wall. He squeezed through, flashing his electric torch.

He found himself in a still larger and higher cave. But there were no paintings here covering the walls. Instead were there tiers and tiers of boxes, hundreds and hundreds of them.

He walked up and examined them. Then he jumped back with a cry of fear and surprise.

The boxes were plainly marked in Tibetan, Hindu, and English—labels which proclaimed that the contents were dynamite and powder and cordite and picric acid and high-power shells of all sorts. They contained every explosive and material for the manufacture of poison-gas and bombs which American and European ingenuity had ever thought or dreamed of.

How much was there? Impossible to guess. But it seemed a great store house, holding doubt-less enough death-giving quantities to blow many regiments of the British-Indian Raj into destruc-tion; and Jimmie knew, from what he had heard in the bazars as well as from what Ghula Khan had told him, how carefully the British guarded the border on their side against gun-running and how even the northern frontiers of Tibet, those parallel with China and Russian Central Asia were continuously supervised by British spies and secret service agents. Yet here were these ex-plosives; and Jimmie said to himself that they must have passed through in dribbles, the result of many years of labor and cunning and efficiency. It made no difference whence they had come—via Pekin or Moscow, Calcutta or Orenburg. They were here and, without a doubt, more would come—to make this place a great armory, perhaps the chief armory, the chief war depot of the Yellow Man, the Tibetan.

Revolution! it was in the making, war and up-heaval and catastrophe—and the ghastly, scarlet promise of a new, yet unwritten page in the Book of History, the Book of Mankind!

Not that Jimmie used these words to himself.
He could not have. He would not have understood their meaning, since he had never read a
newspaper in his life, and since he was unfamiliar
with political slogans and theories. On the
other hand, he had spent his most impressionable
years in the bazars of Chawkpore. He was familiar with their gliding, soft-footed gossip; and
it is this gossip—the low word whispered from
mouth to mouth—which means to India what
newspaper editorials, heavy historical tomes,
stump speeches, propaganda paid and unpaid,
clubs, secret societies, and political associations
mean to the Western world. It was the low
word which, over half a century ago, grew, unknown to, unheard by, the British until overnight
it burst into a storm—the great Indian Mutiny.

And Jimmie had heard, had listened, knew.
The men of the bazars had talked freely in his
presence, since to them he was a native to all in-
tents and purposes. And so he realized that,
while they fought and argued and quarreled on
every other subject under the sun, there was one
on which they all agreed, be they white or brown,
Hindus or Moslems, Causasians by race or Tartars or Dravidians; and this subject was Liberty,
Freedom, Complete Independence from the European yoke.

There was simply no argument about it.   Even

those who had been educated in England, who profited personally by English rule, who had more friends in the British Isles than in Hindustan, who preferred European civilization and ideals and culture to their own—even they, when it came to a final choice, would fight with their own people against the foreigners.   It was in their blood. It was the one thing they dreamed of—the same dream which to their European over-lords spelled nightmare.

They wished and prayed and worked for Liberty as fiercely as Lexington's embattled farmers, as unswervingly as the sons of Erin for a thousand years.   They would obtain it, sooner or later, regardless of the price to be paid in blood and goods, regardless of the consequences.

Perhaps they were wrong.   But, right or wrong, such as their belief.   And Jimmie knew it; knew, too, that when revolution started across the border, it would send its sweeping flames over into India.

And then what?

CHAPTER VI

IT was then that Jimmie understood why the three agents of the C. A. C. C. had disappeared. It was not because of some petty jealousy about trade or haggling about profits, not even because the Dalai Lama did not want the foreigners to defile the Forbidden Land; but lest the agents discover these gigantic preparations for war—war perhaps nurtured and backed by some other Asiatic power or combination of powers, a first skirmish in a great conflict between East and West.

Jimmie had not the book learning he would have accumulated had he gone to an American school. On the other hand his mind had been sharpened to razor-edge by his life in the streets and bazars of Chawkpore. He could put two and two together, and make four out of it—and,

at times, five.   He did not believe that the agents
of the C. A. C. C. had been killed.   He was
certain that the Tashi Lama would not break
his oath.   But he remembered the Afghan having said that, if the Tashi Lama had given such
an oath, had made a point of giving such an oath
by coming down to Darjeeling of his own free
will, he had doubtless done so for a definite purpose, on direct orders from the Dalai Lama in
Lhassa.   Ghula Khan had been right, concluded
Jimmie, putting the bits of information and impression he had gathered together like the pieces
of 'a puzzle-picture.

For Rankin was a prominent man on the
border, chief inspector of the C. A. C. C.,
familiar with many a Central Asian intrigue,
keen, audacious, shrewd, enterprising, a force to
be reckoned with when it came to war, potentially
a very dangerous enemy.   Therefore the Tibetans wanted him out of the way; and so the red-
capped and yellow-capped priests, being clever
students of human nature, thanks to their voca-
tion, had first cradled Rankin into a feeling of
absolute security by the Tashi Lama going to
Darjeeling and giving the oath.   Then they had
played on his American stubbornness by timing
the disappearance of the three practically with his
arrival in Tibet, and by ordering him out of the
country through the *Depon's* warnings and the

monk To Palte's threat, figuring that, the more
the odds seemed against him, the more he would
decide to carry on.

These priests were no fools. Superstitious?
Yes. Also arrogant and provincial. But, after
all, they were clever politicians who knew the human mind, knew how to play with it. They had
figured exactly right.

They must have watched the house in Ya-Tung
while Rankin and his party were there; then,
when the American was alone, must have surprised him. They had kidnapped him, as they
had good reason to want neither bloodshed nor
witnesses. Then, relying on their spy system and
underground information, they had proceeded to
the next step: had got Ghula Khan out of the
way. They had again shown what clever politicians they were. For, besides removing the
Afghan, they had proved their friendliness to the
British-Indian authorities since they returned this
dangerous and much-wanted bandit and gun-
runner into their judicial clutches. Thus they
had discredited ahead of time anything the
Afghan might relate. The British-Indian authorities would simply laugh and refuse to believe
him. Besides, what proof had the Afghan except his bare word—which, naturally, was not
considered gospel-true south of the border.

There remained Jimmie himself. But, thinking, speculating, putting two and two together, he considered that to the Tibetans he was only a native boy, like lots of others, run away from home, picked up in a border bazar, and hardly important to bother about one way or another. Of course they might have thrown him into jail on a trumped-up charge, or without a trumped-up charge. They might have kidnapped him as they had Rankin. They might even have killed him.

But—came Jimmie's next thought—these Tibetans were shrewd. They were thoroughly familiar with the character of the average, bazar-bred Indian. They had doubtless said to themselves that, Hindu as he was to them, he must be by the same token nervous, highly strung, easily panic-stricken; would thus gladly and speedily return to India if given his chance. Then, once home, he would relate there the story of his adventures and spread a wholesome fear of the Forbidden Land in the bazars. It would be a warning to others, including the audacious and inquisitive C. A. C. C. detectives across the passes.

Therefore—the priests must have thought—they had nothing to lose and a great deal to gain by Jimmie's escape back over the border.

Jimmie considered what he should do. For there were two ways for him to take. Either he could endeavor to win through to Chalu as he had intended originally and carry on Rankin's work,

or he could go south, back across the border, and
warn the Indian government.   But sahebs were
difficult men to approach by young bazar boys.
Even if he should gain the ear of one of them,
his story would be doubted.   Of course he might
take along a few of the labels pasted on the boxes
as proof of his grim discovery—or, if not as
proof, then at least as sufficient incentive for the
authorities to order a thorough investigation.

But presently he understood that the latter
alternative to go to India and warn the authorities, was not feasible.   There was the element of
time working against him.   By now the monk,
To Palté, must have discovered his disappearance, must have sent trackers on his trail who
doubtless had found out that he had gone north,
into the hills, instead of south, to escape to India.
Therefore to the monk he was no longer a simple Indian bazar boy, but a potential enemy to
be caught, and the Tibetans would soon be after
him in full cry.   And they were mountaineers
who knew how to travel fast and who, were
familiar with many a short cut and secret path
across the hills.

There was only one way, Jimmie decided.   He
must go forward, to Chalu, and as quickly as
possible.

He told himself that, figuring the direct route
via the Chumbi valley to be a day's march from

Yatung while he had been over two days on the way, he must by now be nearly through the land-slip. For the last few minutes he had noticed that the air was getting less heavy and that there was a steadily growing ray of light, indications that he was nearing the end of the tunnel-like caves. He had no idea what he could do after he reached Chalu. But he must keep on, relying on luck or inspiration.

He sat down to rest for a few minutes. He examined his rifle, saw to it that the trigger worked smoothly, then put the weapon down by his side, careful—as Ghula Khan had taught him —that the muzzle pointed the other way, in back of him, while the butt was parallel with his eyes. He removed his fur-lined *gilgit* felt boots and his heavy, woolen socks, took a can of medi-cated grease from his knapsack, and proceeded to rub his bruised, aching toes with it.

Then he stopped short. He listened.

For, suddenly, from nowhere in particular, he caught the sound of laughter,—laughter, low, mocking, terrible; and the next moment, before he had a chance to rise, to pick up the rifle, or to control his frightened, scattered thoughts, To Palté came around the corner of the cave.

The monk moved forward slowly and negli-gently, one of his long, thin hands which contrasted so strangely with his great bulk outstretched in greeting, the other hand holding a large, businesslike revolver which was leveled straight at Jimmie's head.   On his butter-yellow, moonlike visage was a shining, bland smile of ironic welcome.

"Ah," he purred gently, "so you have decided to proceed farther into my worthless country—to visit unimportant me instead of returning to India as I so courteously begged of you?"

"Oh—" Jimmie made a furious, impotent noise in his throat.   He hated irony more than threats.

"Welcome, friend of my heart!" continued the other, advancing slowly, pitilessly.   "No, no, no, no—" he added rapidly, as his sharp eyes saw Jimmie moving a little to one side—"please keep your seat—a high and glorious seat of much honor, eh?   No, no, no!   I beg of you!   Do not disturb yourself—do not trouble to rise and kowtow, though I am older than you.   What are such trifles as manners between friends who dearly love each other—as you and I love each other?   Never mind the rifle!   Please, soul of my soul!   I am so easily frightened—and I like the muzzle exactly the way it points—away from me!"

He laughed loudly, while Jimmie was silent.

"Have you no word for me?" smiled the monk.

Still Jimmie did not reply.   But, slowly, steadily, he began to collect and dovetail his scattered thoughts.   Presently he was thinking furiously, at

high speed.   He knew that every second counted.
His bare toes wriggled.   They touched the chilly
steel of the rifle barrel, and—at the touch, the
cold surprise of it—an idea came to him, as yet
formless, but commencing to crystalize.

"A guest is as one dearly beloved," went on
To Palté.   "Hospitality is the virtue of the noble
and good.   I am both—noble and good!   I shall
be hospitable to you, little brother.   Come—
speak—give me a small word of gratitude!"

Jimmie hardly listened.   Again he thought;
with every ounce of his inherited American
shrewdness made yet sharper by his life in the
Chawkpore bazars; thought while his toes—as
agile as fingers since for years he had gone bare-
foot—wriggled and twisted, and while the monk
continued mockingly:

"I am so glad you came here!"   He pointed
at the tiers of explosives with a generous, circular gesture.   "You like our little treasure house?
It is yours—everything, everything!   Thus,
splendidly, by giving all our belongings, do we of
Tibet honor our guests.   You must pay me a long
visit.   Stay as long as you please!   No—stay
forever!   Stay until you die!"

Still Jimmie did not reply.   He sat there,
watching the other tensely; thinking, thinking.
His toes wriggled.

"All morning have I waited for the coming of

your feet," To Palté went on blandly. "Twice, impatient, I stepped out on the ledge and into the road, beyond the pools, to watch for you, happily expectant, smoking my little red clay pipe." He laughed. "I came the shorter way—through the Chumbi valley—thinking I would surprise you, my friend. And now—that you are here—" Again he laughed. "Did I not say you might stay here forever—until you die? Assuredly! Tell me—would you prefer dying immediately? Or would you rather have a few minutes so that you can pray to your gods for salvation in the hereafter?"

"Neither!" said Jimmie, spreading his big toe away from the others like a thumb.

"No?"

"No, indeed! For, I believe, the Tashi Lama gave his sacred oath that the lives of the C. A. C. C. agents should be safe!"

"They are safe—quite safe——"

"Then——?"

"You are not an agent of the saheb's company," came the smiling rejoinder. "You see, my friend?"

"Oh yes! I see!" Jimmie's big toe slid a little way up the rifle barrel. "By the way," he asked, "what has happened to the sahebs?"

To Palté laughed. It was rather a vain laugh.

"No reason why I should not tell you, since you are not long for this world. I was taught by a sainted teacher that it is proper to respect the wishes of a dying man. We are keeping the sahebs in a safe place, not very far from here! A place where they have food and drink in plenty and even—for we are kind-hearted, we of Tibet —almost daily in communion with the protective deities of the Chumbi valley. We hope that the deities, and the ministering priests, will be able to persuade them——"

"Persuade them to do what?" asked Jimmie. He was interested as well as fighting for time since the plan in the back cells of his brain had now completely crystallized and was nearing actuality with every wriggle of his bare, agile toes.

"They are wise men," replied the monk. "They know many, many things of the White Man's learning and cleverness—things which we of Tibet have not yet mastered. So we hope to be able to persuade them that, by using this learning and wisdom in the service and for the benefit of the Dalai Lama, great honor will be theirs and also much profit."

"Oh—" sneered Jimmie—"in other words you are trying to make renegades out of them?"

"Renegades?" The monk raised his voice. There was now no irony in his voice. He was utterly sincere. "Renegades no more than Indians, be they Hindus or Moslems, who work for the foreigner, the White Man, the Christian! As you do—you yourself—you—" he grew more angry—"*you* are the renegade—cursed be the mother of your father!" He controlled himself, shrugged his shoulders, and went on: "Yes. We are keeping the sahebs in a safe place and ask them to enter our service. The deities—not to forget the ministering priests—shall give them the choice. If they agree to work for us, there will be the honors and the wealth . . ."

"And if they say no——"

"They will be safely kept——"

"Prisoners?"

"If you wish to call it that!" laughed the monk. "By the way," and he shifted his revolver, drawing a bead straight at Jimmie's heart, "you have not yet told me your preference—" Do you wish to die immediately? Or would you rather first pray to your gods?"

"But—I told you—neither! I am afraid—" Jimmie said unhurriedly—"that I cannot accept your charming hospitality."

"No?"

"No! In fact, I think I shall continue to Chalu and you yourself will show me the way, also seeing that no harm comes to me."

The monk laughed.

"I have often heard tell," he said, "that people about to die at times go mad—through fear."

"Oh—" replied Jim slowly, still fighting for time, "I am not afraid—really!"

"Ah—brave, are you? A very Bengal tiger, eh?"

"Not a bit. I would be afraid if I knew that I was going to die. But . . ."

"But . . ."

"I doubt that I am going to." His big toe curled like a question mark. "In fact I believe that I shall outlive you. It would be a great pleasure to me if I could be present at your burial."

"I have no doubt," replied the other, "nor can I exactly blame you." The man was intensely amused. "But would you mind very much explaining to me the meaning of your exquisite and harmonious words?" he asked ironically.

"Not a bit."

"Very well. Tell me, my young friend."

"I will in a moment," said Jimmie. "But, before I answer *your* question, would you mind answering one of *mine?*"

"Go ahead and ask."

"Then tell me, To Palté—there are many, many death-dealing explosives stored here, aren't there?"

"Yes, my inquisitive friend. And more are coming—more—more!" A look of fanatical sincerity came into the man's oblique eyes. "We have prepared everything, slowly, carefully, and the day will come when we shall strike!" His eyes flashed. "These caves extend for miles—and nearly every week war materials arrive—to be stored away for the coming to the day!"

"All stored here—in these caves, you said?"

"Yes. The landslide is honeycombed—all the way to Chalu, and beneath the city of Chalu. Even now—and we are not ready *yet*—we have enough explosives to blow up half this countryside!"

"And—unguarded?"

"No. Guarded extremely well. For the Tashi Lama himself, he, the earthly incarnation of Srongtsan Gampo, the representative on earth of the Compassionate Spirit of the Mountain, has of late taken up his residence in a temple which opens into the farther end of this tunnel of caves—which sits on top of this tunnel as a seal sits on a letter! His sainted presence is better protection than a million armed men. Too, there are trusted guardians here and there and, as to the other end of the tunnel, the one through which you came, there is my feeble self. There are also the many spies who watch—who watched *you*— all the way from Ya-tung, my friend!"

"I thought so." Jimmie inclined his head. He remembered how, several times, he had had the curious feeling that he was being followed. Then he smiled. "To Palté," he said slowly, "the muzzle of my rifle is pointing away from you——"

"For which praises be to the excellent Lord Gautama Buddha!" smiled the other.

"In fact," went on Jimmie, "it is pointing straight at the boxes of explosives behind me."

"And—?" The monk did not yet understand. But he was slightly puzzled.

"My toe is on the trigger!"

"What?"

"I said that my toe—" he wriggled it—"this one—see! is on the trigger!"

"Oh—" High and shrill soared the monk's cry of baffed rage, "you—" he was about to shoot, thought better of it when Jimmie's low accents told him that it would not help him.

"To Palté," said Jimmie, "my toe pulls the trigger the moment your finger does! And, if I do, if you force me to, up goes this cave in a red whirlwind of fire and death! Packed with explosives, you said? And the Tashi Lama in his temple at the end of the tunnel like a seal on a letter? Enough explosives to blow half the countryside to bits, eh? Consider, To Palté! Consider the cost!"

He was about to shoot

There was a long, tense pause. Finally the monk bowed his head.

"I have considered!" he said.

"And—the result?"

"You win!" came the choked admission.

"Good! And now——"

"Listen! Listen!" the monk cut in feverishly.

"What for?"

"One moment—oh—one moment!"

To Palté talked feverishly. His words rolled out like a stream. Promises—promises of wealth and honors and glory, flattery and cajolery, if Jimmie would but throw in his lot with the people of the Forbidden Land. "You are courageous," he wound up, "you are shrewd, you assuredly are blessed by the gods! Come! Be one of us! The reward will be shining! The honors will be great!

The glory! The Dalai Lama himself will thank you—will reward you if . . ." And, when Jimmie tried to speak—"No, no!" The man was very sincere now. "Consider! You are a Hindu—an Asiatic! Closer you are to us than to these dogs of English! Then why be against us! Why . . ."

"To Palté!" interrupted Jimmie. "I am James Clinton Weatherby, an American and a gentleman. . . ."

"Eh —?" The monk looked up, astonished. "I do not understand!"

Jimmie smiled.

"I didn't think you would. Well—never mind. But—save your breath. I win! And I dictate terms!"

"What terms?"

"First of all—drop your revolver. Push it toward me with your foot—careful—that's it!" Jimmie picked up the revolver with his right hand, still keeping his bare toe on the trigger of the rifle. "Now—turn about! Right!" Jimmie quickly put on his socks and shoes, and rose, revolver in his right, rifle in his left hand. He left his knapsack where it was. "Now—march!"

"Where to?" asked the monk over his shoulder.

"Out of the tunnel—into the temple!"

"No, no, no!"

"Yes, yes, yes!" laughed Jimmie. "You will be my guide! Attempt no treachery! Avoid the other guardians of the tunnel if you can! If you can't you must tell them a plausible lie! The moment you commit treachery—I shall fire— twice! My first shot through your back! My second into the arsenal! Therefore—again— consider the cost!"

"But—" the monk half turned.

"Consider, consider!" insisted Jimmie, swinging his rifle until he had a bead on a box containing half a ton of dynamite.

He waited for the answer.   Finally the monk bowed deeply.

"Follow me!" he said.

CHAPTER VII

THE monk sighed and, for a moment, Jimmie
felt in his heart something akin to pity. He
said to himself that this Tibetan was a patriot,
in his own way, for his own country, his own
ideals, his own judgment of what he thought right
or wrong. He had fought with his own weapons,
and he had lost—while Jimmie had won; had
won so far.

"It was fate, To Palté," he said. "You could
not help it!"

"No! I could not help it!" agreed the monk,
as he led the way up a short flight of stairs into
another cave, high, vaulted, with daylight filter-
ing in from the farther end, tightly packed with
boxes of war material. "Fate—" he mumbled,
as if to himself, "which strikes the high and the
low! *Ahee!* A little, little mouse can gnaw to

134

shreds the elephant's rope fetters—and free
him!"

"And a flea—" laughed Jimmie, thinking of
Ghula Khan's words, "can bite!"

The monk shrugged his shoulders. Typical
of his race, his excitement, his hate, had suddenly
given way to a blighting, withering lethargy, to
that submitting to destiny which is the curse of
Asia.

"It is the Buddha's will," he said.   "Blessed be
the Buddha!   Come!"

They passed through cave after cave, some
completely lined with war supplies, others only
partly, with occasionally a clear stretch of wall,
covered with stucco, white on white, ivory and
snowy enamel skilfully blended with shiny-white
lace, and overlaid with a silver-threaded spider's
web of arabesques, as exquisite as the finest lace,
and of Sanskrit quotations in the ancient deva-
nagari script with ever and again the Dalai
Lama's mystic legend: *"Om ma-ni pad-me!
Hung!"*

They met only one watchman, a gigantic Tibetan captain of the Dalai Lama's guard, who
looked questioningly at Jimmie, with his ragged
clothes and his weapons. The monk's explanation came quick and plausible as Jimmie whispered a warning threat.

"One of my spies," he said, "recently returned

from the border. He has an important message for the Tashi Lama!"

The captain kowtowed deeply at the words.

"Om ma-ni pad-me! Hung!" he exclaimed sonorously, while Jimmie cut in with:

"Is the hour propitious to bow before the Tashi Lama?"

"Yes. The Tashi-Lama—" again the captain kowtowed—"is in the inner hall, alone, meditating as is his custom! Pass in peace!" He stuck out his tongue politely.

They crossed another large cave, one side lined with boxes of explosives, while the other walls, above the white stucco, were painted with a procession, a panorama of conventionalized Tibetan legends and superstitions—from the *Chadanta Jatanka,* the birth-story of the Six-tusked Elephant, the most beautiful of all Buddhistic myths, to the ancient tale of the *Kaliya Damana,* which tells how Krishna overcame the hydra Kaliya; from color-blazing designs picturing the gods Rama, Sita, and Lakshman meditating in their forest exile, to a representation of Bhagiratha imploring Shiva, the Creator, to permit the river Ganges to fall to the earth from his matted locks.

The latter paintings showed an Indian influence as did another large series of fresco that were less of religious and more of historical nature, portraying, in bold, splendid colors, the chief

events of Hindustan, Tibet, and Western and
Northern Central Asia, from the coming of the
Aryans, many thousands of years ago and their
bloody wars with the aboriginal tribes, to the
many invasions—Greeks, Scythians, Arabs, Tartars, Moghuls, Portuguese, straight down to the
British conquest.

Again there were other paintings, rather more
Chinese in character. They were more dainty,
more exquisitely harmonious and charming.

All in all, it told the tale, sublime, sweeping,
eternal, of a nation's glory and martyrdom, a
nation's past life and hopes and achievements,
while, in those many boxes of war supplies, was
told the tale of that same nation's hope for the
future. And the thought came to Jimmie that
perhaps never a White Man had set foot here
before, and he felt like an intruder, felt just a
little afraid. But he shook his head. It was his
duty to carry on, he said to himself, as the monk
stopped in front of a great door set into the farther wall.

"Listen!" said To Palté with a trembling
voice, "listen——"

"What is it?" asked Jimmie.

And again the other's words came in a frothy,
florid stream, imploring Jimmie to throw in his
lot with Tibet, cajoling, flattering, promising
enormous rewards.

"Come!" the monk wound up. "Be one of us! You are shrewd, courageous, clever! How can you resist us? Do you want money? It shall be yours! High office? It shall be yours!"

There was no doubt that the man meant it; and Jimmie was amused—and, too, a little pleased—that, only a very short time ago, he had been nothing but an unimportant bazar boy, an atom in India's swarming life, sent to jail for objecting to an English boy's rudeness. And here he was being treated as an equal—no!—as a superior who could confer favors, whose help was wanted, needed, begged.

But he shook his head.

"Save your breath," he commanded, "and open that door!"

"I will not!" the monk exclaimed stubbornly.

"You will!"

"No, no, no!"

"You must, To Palté! Really—I am sorry—" and Jimmie *was* sorry—"but you must!"

He shifted his rifle a little; his finger moved; there was the sharp, metallic, ominous snick of the breechbolt.

The monk inclined his head.

"*Ahee!*" he sighed. "It is the Buddha's will! We are all of us tied upon the Wheel of Life, the eternal Wheel of Fate! So be it!" He sighed.

Then he looked at Jimmie, an imploring impression in his oblique eyes. "Will you grant me one single favor?" he asked.

"Name it!"

"I am afraid . . ."

"Afraid?"

"Yes," admitted the monk. "Afraid of the Tashi Lama—so very afraid!"

"I am sorry. But you will have to . . ."

"Wait, wait!" interrupted the monk. "I am not asking you for mercy. But three minutes I claim to compose my mind and my spirit, to drive the little devils of fear from my soul, to pray to the Excellent Lord Gautama Buddha!"

"No!"

"Please, please," begged the monk. "What harm is there in it? You have the rifle. I am helpless! Is your heart then made of iron?"

"Very well," finally assented Jimmie. "But— no tricks!"

"What tricks can there be in a short prayer?"

"All right! Go ahead!" said Jimmie, but he did not forget his precautions and kept his rifle at full cock, while the monk prayed, twirling his prayer wheel and rhythmically clicking the wooden beads which it contained.

Click-clock-click said the beads, accompanying the monk's voice which came with a throbbing, low cadence:

"Help me, O Gautama Buddha. Help me, O excellent Tathagata! Let not my soul sink in the slime of fear, O thou Perfectly Awakened One!"

Click—he counted the prayer on the wheel's wooden beads. *Clock!* A short, elusive pause, then, staccato, close together: Click-click-clock, while the voice continued with thick, palpable fervor:

"To enter the Perfect Way without thy help, O Jewel in the Lotus, is impossible!"

Click-clock!

"Help me, help me, O Buddha!"

Clock!

"Permit not fear and passion to enter this heart of mine, uninhabited by meditation and purity!"

Click-clock . . . Clickety-clack——

"Permit me to rise above the world, O Master, even as the wild bird rises from its march to follow the pathway of the sun—" the monk droned on, counting his beads with a dull, staccato rhythm.

Click-clock-click!

Jimmie was growing impatient.

"Come on," he said, "you've prayed enough!"

"One second!" begged To Palté.

Again he whirled his prayer wheel. Again his voice pealed out in an enormous fervor of pious emotion which left Jimmie slightly awed.

"O Jewel in the Lotus!   Help me!" came the monk's prayer.   "Completely, by day and night, my thoughts are fixed upon thy eternal mystery! Unceasingly, by day and by night, the eyes of my soul are fixed upon thy law!   O Thou Perfectly Awakened One!   Help now thy humble disciple to obtain the blessed wakefulness of perfect contemplation.   Let me find force to fulfill my vow! Suffer not evil to prevail against me!   Help me—O Jewel in the Lotus!"

Click!!!

And, with the last staccato thud of the prayer beads, suddenly, with utter rapidity, something came from the back, a great, throttling, crunching force, and descended upon Jimmie's head, shoulder, and arms.   The attack took him absolutely unprepared.   He struggled.   He fought. He tried to pull the trigger of his rifle.   He could not.   The odds were against him.   Twisting his head, turning, he saw that three Tibetan soldiers had rushed up noiselessly from the back, and he understood—too late—that the monk's clicky prayer had been only a call for help, that each thud of the prayer beads had been but the beat of a single code, summoning succor, and it had come, and he—Jimmie—had lost.   One of the soldiers had caught the rifle, had twisted it out of hand, had kicked it into a corner.   Jim-

mie kept on fighting.   But it was hopeless.   A
rough knuckle caught him on the left temple, an
open palm hit the point of his chin.   The monk,
too, joined in the combat until they had pulled
him down as hounds pull down a stag.   A minute
later they had bound and trussed him securely
with ropes and leather straps, and one of the
Tibetan soldiers turned to the monk with a question, asked casually, passionlessly:

"Shall I cut his throat?"

The monk considered, yawned, smiled.

"No," he replied after a pause.   "That is—
not now."

"Dead horses eat no grass," suggested the
other, "and dead men tell no tales.   Don't you
think I had better . . ."

"I know, I know—" interrupted To Palté.
"Dead men tell no tales—right.   But live men
do tell tales—tales, belike, valuable to us of
Tibet, eh?"

"I don't understand," stammered the soldier.

"Don't you?   Ah—I did not think you would!
It is indeed true that he of great head becomes a
priest, and he of great feet a soldier!"   He
turned to Jimmie.   "*You* understand, don't
you?"

Jimmie did not reply, and the monk walked
up to where he lay on the ground.   He patted
him on the hand, and the gesture was quite

friendly, as were the words that accompanied it:

"Perhaps we shall be friends—yet?" he smiled. "Working for the same cause, the same land?" And when Jimmie rejoined with a flow of bitter, picturesque abuse, the other did not seem hurt or angry.

"Do not be a fool, my young friend," he said. "Remember what the ancients advise: 'The hand that thou canst not bite, kiss and put on thy head!" He walked toward the door which led into the temple. "I shall talk to you again—presently."

"Save yourself the trouble!" came the heated rejoinder. "I told you before that I am not going to——"

"To accept a great and shining reward for being one of us?"

"Exactly!"

"How very unreasonable!" Again the monk smiled. "Consider how foolish it is to attempt the impossible. Consider that the little, little tit-mouse cannot push away the elephant with the strength of its back. You are the tit-mouse, and the Dalai Lama is the elephant! Also be pleased to meditate on the fact that, on the egg combating with a stone, the yolk came out. You, my friend, are the egg, and the Dalai Lama is the stone, eh?" He turned to the soldiers. "Put my young friend with the sahebs. Then loosen his bonds. See that he is well treated and fed!" And he disappeared through the door, while one of the soldiers blindfolded Jimmie.

The latter was in a conflicting turmoil of emotions, with rage more than fear uppermost. Active, energetic, impatient of restraint, he hated the bitter realization of absolute helplessness, as he felt himself being picked up, carried along at a rapid trot for six or seven minutes, up and down, heard the protesting creak of a padlock, the opening a door, and finally felt himself pushed into what seemed to be a room where his bonds and blindfold were removed.

The soldiers left. The door slammed behind them. Then, as his eyes became used to the light, he found himself in a room, windowless except for a small, grilled opening high on one of the walls through which a shred of light danced in with reddish mists and weaving a checkered pattern on the grey stone floor. There were several men in the cell, and a moment later one of them rose, stepped forward, and held out a hand.

"Hello!" It was Monro W. Rankin. "There you are, young fellow-my-lad!"

"Oh—Rankin saheb—? stammered Jimmie, half surprised, half relieved.

"Feels good to see a friendly face, eh?" laughed the American. "Come on—and meet the bunch." He waved a hand toward three men who came out of a corner of the room where they had been sitting, playing cards, and who looked like typical grizzled, hard-bitten Anglo-Indians. "Get acquainted with the rest of the C. A. C. C. in this neck of the woods," Rankin continued, introducing the men one by one. "The fellow with the moth-eaten whiskers and the haughty eyes is Bennington. The one with the crop of red hair and the mean swing to shoulders is Thackeray, commonly called Patsy. And the aristocratic gent with the eagle beak and the proud you-go-and-be-hanged manner is old Pedro de Sousa from Goa. And—" putting his arm around Jimmie's shoulders— "This, boys, is Jimmie—beg pardon—Mr. James Clinton Weatherby—of whom you have heard me speak!"

There was a chorus of laughter, of friendly greetings, and they shook hands with Jimmie and made him welcome. They asked Jimmie what had happened, and speculated on their fate when he told them.

"Seems to me we're in no end of a pickle," commented Bennington, "what d'you think we'd better——?"

"Hush!" came Rankin's warning gesture. "Talk lower—and don't talk English!"

"Why not?" demanded "Patsy" Thackeray.

"You'll see why in a moment, you carrot-topped old dunderhead!" And, to Jimmie: "Do our Tibetan friends know that you're an American?"

"I told To Palté so, but it seemed to make no impression upon him."

"Didn't sink in, eh? Well—so much the better! And don't you go and wave the flag again, Jimmie."

"Why not?"

"Because I want the Tibetans to keep on be-lieving that you're a Hindu, a native. So we'd better talk Hindi amongst ourselves."

"But——"

"You see," continued the American, "the Ti-betans made us certain propositions—asked us to throw in our lot with them—allowed that we're valuable birds who know a heap and that we can exchange our knowledge against the coin of the Tibetan realm any time we feel like being good boys——"

"Ah—Santa Maria de Gaudalupe!" exclaimed Pedro de Sousa. "They asked me—*me*, by the Saints!—to become a renegade!"

"Me, too," said Jimmie.

"That's exactly it!" rejoined Rankin. "They think you a Hindu—an Asian—more akin to them, more amenable to reason, less stubborn than a White Man. That's the card you've got to play.   Presently—and don't hurry, take your time, or they'll get suspicious—you're going to let yourself be persuaded and join our red-capped and yellow-capped friends."

"Why should I?"

"For the simple reason that it's the only chance we have of ever getting out of this hole!   For the simple reason that, before I kick the bucket, I want to walk down once more the length of Market Street, and have a look at O'Farrell and the Barbary Coast and Tim Maloney's hash-joint and Tamalpais and the Yosemite and the rest of the California real estate———"

Rankin's patriotic outburst was interrupted by the entrance of servants who brought a generous tray of food, the best of the Tibetan cuisine; a large pot of "buttered tea," a sort of soup made of tea leaves, dough, and clarified butter; un-leavened scones of barley meal; dried cheese; a stew of yak meat, cabbage, and turnips; and, for dessert, a plateful of brown sugar.

They did full justice to their meal; and then, when the servants had left, Rankin put Jimmie through a severe cross-examination.   He laughed when he heard of Ghula Khan's plight, and whis-tled through his teeth when Jimmie told him about the subterranean arsenal.

"Tough on the British Raj!" he commented. "Darned dangerous for the whole western world.

Only—there is one little fly in the Tibetan oint-
ment—isn't there, Bennington?"

"You mean about——"

"Sure—what you overheard when they took
you up to Lhassa to have an interview with the
Dalai Lama, the Tibetan Grand Sachem." And
he explained to Jimmie that, in Lhassa, Bennington, who spoke Tibetan like a native, had chanced
to overhear a conversation between the Dalai
Lama and some of the high Lamaist dignitaries.
The Dalai Lama had lost his temper. "Very
well!" he had exclaimed. "It will be as you
wish! War—strife—the shedding of blood!
You want it—you priests and abbots and
monks— But I——"

"That's all Bennington heard," continued Rankin. "But it shows which way the wind blows.
It shows that there's a difference of opinion up at
Lhassa and that the Dalai Lama doesn't deem to
be exactly tickled to death with the fighting
monks—see, Jimmie?"

"Yes," said the latter. "But the Tashi Lama
was only obeying the Dalai Lama when he came
down to Darjeeling and gave the oath by which
he inveigled you into the hills. That's what
Ghula Khan said!"

"And that Afghan roughneck was doubtless
right!"

"Then—what——?"

"Perhaps the priests forced the Dalai Lama's hand! Perhaps—well—I don't know! But that's just what we have to find out. Now roll up and go to sleep, boy. You'll need all your nerve by'n-by!"

And Jimmie stretched himself out in a corner and was soon asleep.

"I raise that pot two rupees!" was the last thing he heard. "I'll show you how we play poker in San Francisco—here—pot's mine, I guess—full of aces, boys——"

CHAPTER VIII

"I HOPE that your sleep has refreshed you?"
Jimmie awakened to find To Palté standing over him.

"Thanks," he replied.

"Be pleased to accompany me," the other went on.

Jimmie stretched himself, yawned, and rose.

"Where to?" he asked.

"To the Tashi Lama. He will see you. What is your name?"

Jimmie laughed.

"That's right," he commented. "You never asked me."

"No," came To Palté's reply; and he smiled, rather good-humoredly. "At first I did not consider you important enough to ask your name, and afterwards—Buddha, Buddha!—I was, be-

like, too, frightened—when you threatened me
with your rifle."

Jimmie took the first Hindu name that popped
into his head—name as common in India as Smith
or Brown in America.

"I am Chandra Das," he replied, as he turned
to go.

As he neared the threshold he heard Rankin's
stage whisper. He was talking to Bennington,
in Hindi, so that To Palté might understand and
draw conclusions—wrong conclusions, he hoped.

"Can't trust those Hindus," he said. "I befriended that young Chandra Das, didn't I?
Well—two to one he sells out to the Tibetans."

"What do you expect?" rejoined Bennington,
also in Hindi and in a stage whisper. "A Hindu
is always a Hindu—with his courage in his stomach, his loyalty in his purse, and his anger on the
edge of his nose. Yes, yes—" he sighed—
"The mule's friendship is kicking!"

"All alike, these White Men, these sahebs,
aren't they, Chandra Das?" smiled the monk as
he took Jimmie across the threshold and down
the length of a dimly lit corridor. "They hate
and despise us—the people of Asia. Did you
hear what they said?"

"I did."

"Don't you think that I am right?" insisted To
Palté.

"No!"

"Then you are a fool—a blind, deaf fool! These sahebs—you heard yourself what they said about you and your people, your race, your land!"

Jimmie shook his head. He remembered Rankin's advice not to hurry, to take his time, lest the other should become suspicious.

"I have no quarrel with the Raj," he said. "And I am grateful to Rankin saheb."

"Ah!" smiled the monk. "Are you forgiving your enemies? Are you practicing, belike, the weak Christian virtue of turning your left cheek when your enemy smites your right?"

"Rankin saheb is my friend," Jimmie insisted stubbornly.

"Oh yes," sneered To Palté. "He cherishes the shadow of your feet as Paracarika cherished Sakha, the god of ruddy color! And yet—did he not say that all Hindus are alike? Did he not say that you would sell out to us?"

By this time they had reached the farther end of the corridor where a great door, inlaid with ivory and colored enamel, barred the way. To Palté opened it. Then, as soon as he had crossed the threshold, threw himself flat on the ground touching it with his forehead and his hands, while Jimmie looked up.

He saw a very small, circular room, its walls

covered with slabs of delicate carving that was like sculptured embroidery and, in the centre, on a simple chair of black wood, a shriveled old man in a plain robe of yellow wool, with neither jewels nor ornaments. Jimmie gave an involuntary shudder as he saw the face, wrinkled, brown, immobile on a scrawny neck which was like the slimy stalk of some poisonous jungle flower, as he felt the staring, blinking, unhuman eyes boring into his.

"*Om ma-ni pad-me!*" mumbled the monk.

"*Om ma-ni pad-me! Hung!*" echoed the other. "Rise, To Palté!"

The monk obeyed. He turned to Jimmie. "The Tashi Lama!" he whispered in his ear; and, kowtowing deeply before the high-priest: "I have brought the young Hindu of whom I spoke, Heaven-Born. Chandra Das is his name!"

"Chandra Das!" repeated the Tashi Lama. "A good Hindu name—a name belonging to an ancient, civilized race—race that was peaceful and powerful and prosperous before the White Man came, bringing strife and hate and bloodshed—ah! Come, Chandra Das! Step forward!"

Jimmie obeyed and, for several minutes, the Tashi Lama stared at him, closely, scrutinizingly, while Jimmie felt something like a current of

eerie superstition flow over his soul as he thought
that this wrinkled old man was supposed to be
the earthly incarnation of Srongtsan Gamp, the
representative on earth of the Compassionate
Spirit of the Mountain, almost a Buddha, second
in rank only to the Dalai Lama himself, whose
divine names and many titles were uttered with
devotion throughout Tibet, Mongolia, Ladak,
and the Himalayan States down to Bothan, and
from Lake Baikal in Russian Siberia to Western
China, to the very gates of Peking.

"I heard about you," the Tashi Lama continued presently. "To Palté told me. Clever you
are—eh? and quick-witted and courageous—
charming, charming!" For a few seconds he was
silent. His right hand disappeared into the
loose sleeve of his robe and brought out a
wooden prayer wheel. He twirled it rapidly.
Then he smiled. "And you won—very nearly—
eh, Chandra Das? Down there in the tunnel
you were the victor. Your finger was on the
trigger of your weapon. One shot! And there
would have been ruin and destruction! Then To
Palté prayed. He clicked his wooden beads as
I am clicking these. Hayah!" The Tashi
Lama laughed—"great indeed is the power and
strength of a prayer fervently uttered, fervently
clicked, for help came, and now you are here,
helpless, eh? Ashamed—ridiculous—just like

the mule that went seeking for horns and lost its ears!"

Again he laughed loudly, and the monk joined in the merriment.

The Tashi Lama turned to the latter.

"You said that Chandra Das, being so clever and quickwitted and courageous, is doubtless not without honor amongst the sahebs? That, being perhaps as quickeared as he is quickwitted, he overheard, belike, some of their plans—plans which might be valuable to Tibet?"

The monk kowtowed deeply.

"Yes, Heaven-Born!"

"And—you suggested to our young friend Chandra Das that we of Tibet are generous in rewarding our friends?"

"Yes, Heaven-Born!"

"You also suggested to him that we are harsh in punishing our foes?"

"Indeed, Heaven-Born!"

"Good, good!" Once more the Tashi Lama addressed Jimmie. "What is your answer, my friend?"

"My answer is No!"

"You are quite sure of that?"

"Quite!"

"Why, Chandra Das?"

"The sahebs are my friends!"

"Loyal, eh?"

"Yes."

"Yes, yes.   Loyalty is a most charming virtue, especially recommended by the excellent Lord Gautama Buddha!   But tell me: should not the sword cut both ways?   Should not the sahebs be as loyal to you as you are to them?   And, if they are not, would it not be wise to consider that the food of the tiger brings indigestion to the wolf, and that it is useless to carry water in a sieve? The sahebs, you say?   Hayah!"   Suddenly a note of ringing sincerity leaped into the Tashi Lama's voice.   "They are not your friends, by Buddha and by Buddha!   For they *are* sahebs—and you are a Hindu, an Asian!   They have stolen your country—as they want to steal mine!"

"They have paid me well and treated me well."

"Pah!   They have paid you with what they stole from your own country.   When the dogs are sated, they are generous with what remains! No, no—they are thieves, robbers.   But even the fleetest horse cannot escape its own tail.   Now the whirlwind is upon them.   For we—of Tibet, we of the North, we of all Asia—are gaining strength every day.   Why don't the sahebs stay in their own land?   Is it not true that every man should sweep the snow in front of his own door before busying himself with the frost on his neighbor's tiles?   Then let the sahebs sweep

their own snow!   Let them not meddle with the
destinies of the Yellow and the Brown!   And
when they do meddle, when they are caught in
the act of meddling, then let them pay the cost
and bear the punishment!   Come—be one of
us, Chandra Das!   Do not turn your face away
from your own people in the hour of need—
when every last bit of information we can gather
may be of value—may help us to achieve liberty
and power and happiness!"

Jimmie had listened carefully; had considered
as carefully.   He told himself that he was here
in the role of Chandra Das, an average young
bazar-bred Hindu.   He would have to act as a
real Chandra Das would under the circumstances.
Doubtless, he decided, such a one would be in-
fluenced by the Tashi Lama's words, not only
through the implied flattery, but also because
deep in every Hindu's heart is a latent, strong
patriotism, a latent, strong hate against all Europeans.   Yes! the real Chandra Das would be
carried away by the Tibetan's words.   Not only
that.   For there was also other reasons, dove-
tailing with his plans, why he should appear to
be swayed by the Tashi Lama's impassioned ap-
peal.   So he said to himself that the proper moment had arrived to give in a little—a little, but
not too much.

"Yes, yes," he mumbled to himself, but loud

enough to be understood, and watching the Tashi Lama tensely from beneath lowered eyelids as a mongoose watches a cobra, to see the effect of his words. "I, too, am an Asian—I am an Oriental—and——"

"Indeed!" boomed out the Tashi Lama.

"Indeed! Glory be to the Excellent Buddha!" chimed in To Palté.

"Chandra Das," went on the Tashi Lama, "it is true. We are—all, all—the sons of Asia, the Great Mother! And the sahebs are our enemies! We—all of us, Rajputs, Tibetans, Chinese, Japanese, Hindus, Tartars, Moors, Manchus, Arabs, or Turks, Malays or Burmese or Siamese—we have conquered them before, and we shall conquer them again. We shall give them a land hissing with blood and the sword when it is red! We shall drive them as the wind drives a thin sheet of flame, relentless, resistless!"

But when again he pressed Jimmie to tell him whatever he might have found out from Rankin and the C. A. C. C. agents, promising him a great reward, and winding up with "Come! Kneel before me! Swear fealty to our cause!" Jimmie decided that he had better fight for time; he shook his head.

"No," he said, "Not yet!"

"But—a moment ago you agreed that I am

right—that you, too, are an Asian—that our in-
terests are alike——"

"Yes—but——"

"What?" demanded the Tashi Lama impatiently.

"I need time to think—to reflect——"

"There is nothing to reflect about! The issue is clear! Tell me—now!"

"No!"

"Why not, stubborn boy?"

"Because—though there are things I found
out amongst the sahebs—important things——"

"Ah!"

"Yet shall I not tell them to you!" continued
Jimmie watching the effect of his words on the
other's face. "I shall tell them only to one
man!"

"Namely?"

There was a pause. Then the Tashi Lama
smiled a thin smile.

"Chandra Das," he said, with something like
admiration in his accents, "you are indeed a
Hindu, twin-brother to the grey-wolf, clever and
shrewd. You are right! Never tell the cat
what you can tell the tiger! Never take silver
when you can get gold! Very well! It will be
as you wish! You shall tell the Dalai Lama
himself!" He turned to the monk. "To
Palté!"

"Heaven-Born?"

"We start for Lhassa today—immediately. See that the caravan is made ready! Send quick runners ahead to tell Lhassa of our coming!"

The monk kowtowed.

"Listen is to obey, Heaven-Born! What are your orders as to the sahebs?"

"We will take them along. And you, Chandra Das, shall travel by my side, as my honored guest." Again he turned to the monk. "Hurry, To Palté!"

"Wait—" said Jimmie as the monk was about to leave the room.

"What is it?" asked the Tashi Lama.

"Let me spend a few minutes with the sahebs before we start on our journey."

"Why—?" came the suspicious question.

Jimmie thought rapidly, shrewdly.

"Because," he replied, "perhaps, by telling them that you offered me a great reward if I would turn against them, by telling them furthermore that I refused, that in spite of threats and cajoleries I remained loyal to them, they might trust me even more, give me yet more of their confidence!"

"Good, by the Buddha!" laughed the Tashi Lama. "You are blood-brother to the snake, my Chandra Das! You are right! Give the sahebs the stinking oil of flattery, and they will throw away the scabbard of precaution!"

He blessed Jimmie with three fingers, with a deep-throated: *"Om ma-ni pad-me! Hung!"* and, a few minutes later, Jimmie had rejoined Rankin and the C. A. C. C. agents and told them what had happened.

Rankin laughed.

"Played poker with the old bird and bluffed him to a standstill?" he commented. "Well, I guess it's your American heritage. I always did hold that you can't learn to play poker—you got to be born with it—it's hereditary, like rolling your own. But—what are you going to do when you see the Number One Ace High Grand Muckamuck, the Dalai Lama himself?"

"Play poker again," smiled Jimmie, "Anyway—I always wanted to get a look at Lhassa!"

Half an hour later the monk called again for Jimmie and took him into another room where he fitted him out from head to toe in Tibetan costume—"since," he smiled, "you are going to be one of us—perhaps——"

"Perhaps!" Jimmie smiled in return; but he was glad to exchange his torn, travel-stained garments for warm, home-spun trousers, cloth boots, a garnet-colored, furlined coat and a fur cap turned up with a yellow brim. Nothing was forgotten to make of him a Tibetan dandy, not even the prayer wheel and rosary, the large gold-filigree amulet box shaped like a breastplate and picked out with great pieces of amber and coral and, in his left ear, a long ear ring with pearl and turquoise pendant sweeping down to his shoulder.

They were off for the North within the hour, passing along the Chumbi valley trail beneath a bright, cloudless sky, past Kala and Samada toward Gyantse.

Rankin and the three C. A. C. C. agents were on horseback, closely guarded by a troop of Tibetan cavalry. The latter were a ruffianly-looking lot, in their uniforms of grey homespun woolen with red and blue collars and with accoutrements that smacked of the Middle Ages. For they wore iron helmets ornamented with peacock feathers, cuirasses of small, narrow, willow-like steel leaves threaded with leather thongs, while the high officers wore chain-mail and clothed even their horses in armor. The riding-gear was a blaze of barbaric splendor, with saddle-carpets cf scarlet and yellow embroidered with purple and green, throat tassels of crimson and gold, high peaked saddles, massive bits and stirrup-irons inlaid with silver and gold. The weapons, too, were medieval; spears, ugly, two-edged swords, bows and arrows, the latter of bamboo with wicked iron heads three inches long, battle axes, and heavy shields of yak-hide with iron bosses. A few carried triangular banners, with tufts of yak-hair dyed crimson and blue.

But the infantry which followed was armed with modern rifles, and so was the Tashi Lama's body-guard which surrounded the latter's palanquin, a gorgeous affair and in which rode the Tashi Lama, with Jimmie by his side.

The former was deep in the study of a Tibetan book, an almanac for the year. He showed it to Jimmie, explaining the grotesque symbols and terms of which it was composed: the five basic elementals, wood, fire, earth, iron, and water, and the zodiacal beasts corresponding to the twelve-year cycle of Tibetan reckoning.

"Eleven," he said, "are the beasts of ill-omen, the years of ill-omen! Sheep, ape, bird, dog, pig, mouse, ox, tiger, serpent, hare, and horse! But this is the lucky year of the Wood-Dragon! See what it says in the prophecy!" And he read from the almanac: "In the year of the Wood-Dragon the first part of the year protects the Jewel in the Lotus; there comes then a great thronging of robbers, quarreling and fighting, many enemies, troublous grief by weapons and such like will arise, also danger of red conflict with the foreigner, and spying and telling of lies here and there!" The Tashi Lama shook his head.   "The almanac speaks the truth," he commented.   "Trouble there enough—with the sahebs' agents overrunning the land like vermin in an old coat—and spying enough, with the sahebs' spies here and there and everywhere— *ahee!*"   Again he turned to the almanac, reading aloud: "But, before the end of the year, if the beasts of the zodiac be mollified there might yet come a conciliatory sending from a foreign land; a youth to give a true and shining nimbus to the Jewel in the Lotus, and to bring victory!"

He was silent: thought deeply: then, suddenly, sat up straight, tense, excited.

"Hayah!" he cried.   "A conciliatory sending from a foreign land—a youth to give a true and shining nimbus to the Jewel in the Lotus—perhaps—perhaps it is you, Chandra Das, who——"

He interrupted himself, thrust open the curtains of yellow silk.

"Hurry!" he shouted to the leader of the caravan men.   "Hurry!"

"Yes, Heaven-Born!"

CHAPTER IX

THEY traveled all the afternoon, resting at
night at Samada and continuing early the
next morning along a deep, gloomy ravine
where the cold was intense, between steep cliffs
that rose to a height of sixteen and seventeen
thousand feet, on through a gorge where the valley had contracted into a narrow cleft through
which the river gurgled noisily, dashing and tumbling over the huge rocks fallen from the cliffs
above. Here the elevation was about fourteen
thousand feet, and they passed again into the
zone of shrubs, with dwarf red junipers thickly
dotting the peaked summits of the hills.

The next night they rested in the Na-nying,
the "Monastery of the Ancient Ear," and were
off before the sun had shot up behind the hills.

For—"Hurry, hurry!" was the Tashi Lama's eternal command.

Lower down they emerged from the rocky defiles on to a fertile, well-cultivated sweep of alluvial lands with flourishing villages.   At one of them the headman came out to pay his respects to the Tashi Lama.   He wore the fluffy tam o' shanter of yellow wool which all Tibetan laymen must put on when talking to a Lama or high official, bowed courteously with out-thrust tongue, and offered in his extended hands a ceremonial scarf of yellow, embroidered silk.

But the Tashi Lama hardly listened to him. He was impatient.

"Hurry!   Hurry!" he called to his retinue.

And they hurried, down along the broad meadows of the Nyang river fringed with willow bushes amongst which hopped swarms of great Tibetan magpies, black and white, with glossy green tails, chattering almost as loudly as the caravan men; then up again, to an elevation of nearly sixteen thousand feet, amongst huge, piled-up boulders, studded with fiery patches of scarlet-leaved barberry bushes.

The Tashi Lama did not speak much to Jimmie.   He seemed nervous, occupied with his thoughts, laboring under some great, voiceless excitement, reading and re-reading his almanac, twirling his prayer wheel, mumbling uncounted

"*Om ma-ni pad-me!   Hung's!*" and occasionally carrying on whispered conversations in the "secret" language, the sacred language of the Lhassa abbots which Jimmie did not understand, with the red-capped and yellow-capped priests who spurred their ponies alongside the palanquin.

Always was there a referring to the almanac, always quick, significant glances in the direction of Jimmie.

They were joined in the monastery by a runner who had come up from the south.   The Tashi Lama listened to what the man had to say, then turned to Jimmie.

"There is trouble beyond the border, Chandra Das," he said.   "The British are threatening. There is danger.   We are not yet fully prepared. And yet—" he shook his head, pointed at the almanac—"this *is* the year of the Wood-Dragon! And—" he interrupted himself, rose, called over to To Palté.

"To Palté!"

"Heaven-Born?"

"We must hurry!"

"Listen is obey, Heaven-Born!"

So they were off again, and early the following afternoon Gyantse, the halfway station to Lhassa, came fully into view, in the midst of a broad valley that fingered up to the granite of the hills, with hardly any snow on the ground, a steadily rising temperature, a soft wind blowing from the west; with neat, white-washed farm houses and villas clustering in groves of birch and poplar trees amongst well-cultivated fields and, towering high above, the glistening, white fort of Gyantse, bold and grim and impregnable.

The caravan entered Gyantse amidst boisterous shouts of welcome, the townspeople running from their houses, laughing and yelling. For many of the soldiers and caravan men had friends and relatives living here, and so there was chaos and excitement and noise; comrades greeting each other with embraces and a flow of queries which neither party seemed to think of answering; inferiors recognizing monks from their home villages by sticking out their tongues politely; a huge, fat old Tibetan woman, in a greasy, ruby colored felt robe and laden with coral and turquoise jewelry, running around a tall mule on top of which her six-foot son sat enthroned across a high bale of baggage, she weeping for joy, he bending double in a vain effort to kiss her; noise and confusion; the animals stumbling and tripping; men jumping from horses and mules and running into a plotted square where the bazar was held, anxious to buy a few luxuries after the hardship of the long trek; laughing, haggling.

Jimmie asked permission to stretch his legs and, accompanied and watched by a soldier, he took a

look at the place—the first large Tibetan town
which he had seen. It was market day, and so
the narrow streets were crowded with men in flow-
ing, cherry-colored coats astride lean ponies,
which they flicked with their dog-whips; lines of
donkeys plodding in single file with loads of grain
or fodder; slatternly women, carrying baskets
with food or children slung on their backs or riding astride their broad hips. The houses were
stone-built, mostly two-storeyed, with wooden,
gaily painted balconies facing the tortuous main
streets whence narrow lanes struck off into reek-
ing, uninviting slums. The houses of the wealthy
were distinguished by their windows covered with
transparent, crimson Chinese paper, and by the
printed, sacred texts and charms pasted over the
doors.

The large market square was packed with ped-
lars and traders, tall, hulking, oblique-eyed men
with hook noses, their weather-beaten, broad, unwashed faces brightened by turquoise ear rings,
their pig-tailed locks capped by fur-lined felt hats
with turned-up ear lappets, shod in boots made of
bright-red cloth, their greasy, cherry-colored
coats girdled at the waist like dressing-gowns,
and hitched up to form capacious, impromptu
breast pockets. From these pockets they pro-
duced odds and ends of things for sale, while they
devoutly fingered the beads of their rosaries with

the other hand. There were also a few Chinese traders, lording it over the Tibetans and over the "Kokos," the half-breed descendants of Chinese who had married Tibetan wives. Furthermore, there were local priests, loafing through the market, fingering various things, and evidently helping themselves to what pleased them without payment.

Decidedly—Jimmie thought—it paid to be a Buddhist priest in Tibet!

He was interested and amused, but he did not have time to stay long. For a trumpet was blown as a signal to gather and be off.

"Hurry! Hurry!" was the order.

"We are off to Lhassa today!" said the Tashi Lama. "The year of the Wood-Dragon, the lucky year!"

"The animals are tired," objected the monk.

"Get fresh ones!"

"The people, too! Grant them a day's rest, Heaven-Born!"

"You have heard my orders. We are off to Lhassa today!"

The monk kowtowed.

"Listen is obey, Heaven-Born."

During the entire journey Jimmie had caught no more than a glimpse here and there of Rankin and the C. A. C. agents, although frequently, under pretext of stretching his legs, he left the

palanquin and walked on foot for a mile or two.
And when he suggested to the Tashi Lama that
it might be worth while for him to spend a few
hours in their company to see if they would give
him more of their confidence, the other shook
his head.

"No, he said, "By this time they must know
that you are friendly to me. Hayah! One lie
in a saheb's beard will keep out twenty truths!"

But, during the short halt at Gyantse, he managed to near the group where the prisoners were
being guarded by the Tibetan cavalrymen. The
caravan men were busy levying fresh mounts, the
other soldiers were mostly in the bazar, the
Tashi Lama was deep in conversation with To
Palté and a number of Gyantse abbots, and so
for the moment nobody was watching.

The cavalrymen, ignorant peasants from the
North, had been left to their own devices while
their officers were buying opium balls at the bazar. They stuck out their tongues politely and
kowtowed as Jimmie approached their group.
They knew that he had ridden in the Tashi
Lama's palanquin, saw his resplendent Tibetan
costume, and imagined doubtless that he was the
scion of some aristocratic, priestly Lhassa clan.

Jimmie sat down and told Rankin and the
others in a whisper the few things that had happened since they had left Chalu, chiefly the Tashi

Lama's remark about the almanac and the year of the Wood-Dragon.

He is quite wrapped up in that almanac of his," he added, "speaks a lot about—I remember the exact words—'the conciliatory sending from a foreign land—the youth to give a true and shining nimbus to the Jewel in the Lotus.' He seems to connect me, somehow, with the Prophecy——"

"What do you imagine the old bird is driving at?" asked Rankin.

"I have no idea," replied Jimmie.

It was Bennington, thoroughly familiar with Tibetan customs and legends, who proposed an explanation.

"The Tibetan year," he said, "is different from ours. It goes by twelve-year and sixty-year cycles. The present year—the year of the Wood-Dragon—is nearly over—in a few weeks. That's why he is in such a hurry to get to Lhassa."

"Just as clear as pea-soup!" commented Rankin. "I don't get you, kind sir!"

"Don't you?" Bennington laughed. "These Tibetans are a superstitious lot—the Tashi Lama as much as the rest of them, and they put a great faith in their almanacs and the prophecies they contain." He turned to Jimmie. "Something about a youth from a foreign land giving a true and shining nimbus to the Jewel in the Lotus, didn't you say?"

"Yes—and something, too, about it happening before the year is out."

"Right. And the year is nearly out—and that's why he is in such a confounded hurry."

"Yes, yes," Jimmie cut in excitedly. "The Tashi Lama is nervous. Back at the Na-nying a runner came up with news that the British are beginning to make a fuss."

"Why—" said Bennington—"it's quite clear. There is no doubt in the world but that——"

His further words were interrupted by the braying of the long war-trumpets, a shrill command to up-saddle and be off, and Jimmie hastened back to the palanquin.

A few minutes later, the caravan jingled away on the road to Lhassa.

Lhassa! The Forbidden Town! The Seat of the Gods! The home of the Dalai Lama, the Jewel in the Lotus, the Living Buddha! And, with every step of the way, Jimmie became more conscious of a tremendous excitement that gripped him almost physically. As he traveled on beneath the glistening northern sky that changed the higher hills into glowing heaps of topaz, that painted the ridges into carved masses of amethyst and rose-red, he felt a prey to a curious sensation, with an accent in it of something very ancient and very remote, of a secret dread, of a terrible, secret melancholy as if this far land of Tibet, undefiled these many centuries by the foot of the foreigner, untouched these many centuries behind its snowy Himalayan ramparts by contact with foreign civilization and progress, were bemoaning the sending of fate which, sooner or later, would throw its stony gates wide open to the invasion of a modern era. Jimmie felt it, somehow. The terror of a mighty struggle was behind it; a mighty struggle awfully remote from individual existence and individual ambition and life, individual death even. It partook of Tibet itself; the hills, the land, the ancient race, the ancient superstitions and prophecies—the very gods, the Buddha!

And a whisper seemed to drift down from the north, from Lhassa; a whisper to hurry, hurry— as the trail led past ragged hills that looped to the east in a stony tide of grey, sinister immensity, through the gaunt shadows of the low, volcanic ridges that trooped back to the Indian border and danced like hobgoblins among the dwarf oaks and acacia shrubs.

From Gyantse the road led northeast, past Boghzi, the so-called "Four Doors,"' where four important caravan tracks converge, and through the gorge of the Balung river, and on through the "Valley of Horns" to the fertile upper table land of central and northern Tibet, bounded by rolling downs and grassy uplands, stretching up, fanwise,

to the dark-red sandstone hills, covered in part
with pastures of deepest emerald green, and un-
derfoot a springy turf that was a vivid embroidery of pink primulas, blue, striped gentians, co-
balt and poppies, and over all the fragrant scent
of worm wood. Here and there small hamlets
lined the alluvial bottoms on both banks of the
stream, with a good deal of cultivation, mostly
mixed barley and peas with occasional bright yellow patches of mustard, the houses being painted
vertically in broad stripes of red and blue. Farther on they passed through Ta-klung, the "Tiger's Valley," so-called from its framing of black
limestone rocks streaked with light-yellow sandstone.

That night they made camp in the Ta-t'ang,
the "Horses' Plain," in a cluster of caves made by
prehistoric men, where they were joined by runners, both from the south and from Lhassa, who
talked to the Tashi Lama excitedly in the "secret"
language of the Lhassa abbots. There seemed
to be a violent difference of opinion between the
southern runners and those from the capital,
quelled by the Tashi Lama who, as on the former
occasion, pointed, as if in proof of his contention,
at the almanac and then, with a low, muttered
word, at Jimmie—Jimmie who, boyishly, clear
through his own excitement and faint misgivings
of fear and apprehension, enjoyed the sensation

of importance which he seemed to be causing.

They were off again beneath a driving rain storm, stopping the next day for a short noon rest in a mountain-monastery and temple, dedicated to Dorjé Pa'gmc, the "Pig-faced Goddess," a reincarnation of the "Thunderbolt Saw" divinity of Buddhist myths which, according to the Tibetan legends, was the wife of a demoniacal sort of centaur, the "Horse-necked Tamdin," and was given with him the joint task of defending Buddhism against its enemies.

The temple, surmounted by a great Chinese pagoda, was a square building with a porch on which were ranged, as protecting angels, the colossal, leering figures of the four mythological guardian kings, clad in mail armor of ancient Chinese pattern, each bearing a special emblem and painted a different color: the complexion of the guardian of the East, of the rising sun, white as the dawn of young morning; the guardian of the West, of the setting sun, a golden color; and the Northern, who presides over the realm of ice, a cold green.   Flanking these giant statues were rows of stone-images, painted dark blue, and representing devils and many-headed giants.   Inside, the building was a mass of prayer flags: "Banners of Victory" circular and made of black yak hair banded with crosses of white: huge gilt banners with the symbolic *"Om ma-ni pad-me!*

Hung!" triangular silken streamers, symbolic of the Buddhist trinity, and crimson flags painted with the "Wheel of Life."

In the central assembly hall, as usual in Tibetan temples, sat enthroned on a gilt lotus stool a living incarnation of the presiding deity, of the "Pig-faced Goddess," a tiny, six-year-old girl child who stared upon the world at large and the praying Tashi Lama out of uncomprehending, morose eyes while the priests walked about, chanting and swinging golden incense-burners that swirled up with clouds of scented smoke, darkening the air with solid, bloated shadows, wreathing everything in floating vapors of crimson and grey.

But if the little girl who was the deity seemed mute and uncomprehending, perhaps dreaming of toys and childish games, there was no doubt of the Tashi Lama's tremendous sincerity of purpose, as he kowtowed deeply before her, begging her to intercede for him with her spiritual ancestors—*"Om ma-ni pad-me! Hung!"* he cried fervently. "Cause thou the strong charioteer of resolve not to lose control over the wild team of fear! Help thou thy humble disciple to obtain the blessed wakefulness of perfect strength! Let him find force to fulfill his destiny! *Hung!"* —as he asked Jimmie to kneel by his side and join in his prayers.

"Come, Chandra Das!" he said.   "You are one of us!"

When Jimmie hesitated, embarrassed, non-plussed, feeling somehow sorry for the man, the latter repeated, anxiously, almost imploringly:

"You are one of us.   Tell me that you are. Hayah!   The year of the Wood-Dragon is draw-ing to its close, and the beasts of the zodiac are not yet mollified!   There is trouble on the south-ern border.   Daily the sahebs are growing more impatient, and we are not yet ready for the test-ing of strength—not yet ready—ahee!"

CHAPTER X

THE news of the sahebs' impatience was confirmed by another emissary who came thundering up the valley on his tough little hill pony, spurring it on unmercifully, jumping off as he neared the temple, rushing in without ceremony and scattering the priests as a wind scatters chaff.

Jimmie recognized him as Kyu-go, the *Depon,* the governor of the Chumbi valley, who had met Rankin at Ya-tung and had warned him, either out of honest friendship or, acting under orders from Lhassa, so as to play on Rankin's American stubbornness, to return post-haste to India. The last time he had seen Jimmie, the latter had been dressed in rough mountaineering clothes, his face hid by Balaklava cap and woolen scarf; now he did not seem to recognize him beneath his gorgeous raiment, and Jimmie was glad of it.

"It is not proper to disturb a man at prayer and meditation," said the Tashi Lama reprovingly.

"I know it," replied the Depon, speaking, since he was a man of the military caste and thus unfamiliar with the abbots' "Secret" language, in the ordinary Tibetan which Jimmie understood. "But—things happened——"

"What things?"

The Depon pointed a significant thumb at Jimmie, but the Tashi Lama who, under that blighting superstition which is the curse and the weakness of half Asia, had become daily more certain that Jimmie was the "conciliatory sending from a foreign land" of which the almanac spoke, told him to continue.

"Well, Kyu-go?"

"Ghula Khan!" said the other.

Jimmie looked up, intensely interested.

"What about him?" asked the Tashi Lama. "We arranged everything most carefully! Doubtless there, by delivering into the sahebs' hands a dangerous ruffian wanted for gun-running and the many other crimes, we proved ourselves friends of the Raj!"

"It seems that we forgot one thing, Heaven-Born!" "Namely?"

"The ancient saying that it is unwise to trust an

Afghan before a snake! The ancient saying
that an Afghan can steal food from between your
lips, without your stomach knowing it! The ancient saying that an Afghan may be nothing today—but that tomorrow he may be fire and
storm! The ancient saying that——"

"Enough of ancient sayings!" cut in the Tashi
Lama impatiently. "Give me straight talk, bab-
bler! What happened?"

"The Buddha," said the Depon, "made perfect
three things: the saheb's brain, the hand of the
Chinese, and the tongue of the Afghan!"

"'Go on, go on!" cried the Tashi Lama, growing angry.

The other bowed.

"First," he continued, "Ghula Khan lied his
head into the hangman's noose, and then he lied
himself out again, though—" he gave a crooked
smile—"he did not lie exactly, at that! Confidential messengers brought word from beyond
the border that he succeeded in obtaining an interview with Sir Hector McMahon——"

"You mean—" came the Tashi Lama's excited
query—"the commander-in-chief of the Raj's ar-
mies?"

"The same! He saw Ghula Khan; spoke to
him. My spies brought me word."

"And what happened?" demanded the Tashi
Lama. "Go on, slow-witted son of a devil!"

The Depon flushed, but kept his temper.
Again he bowed. "Ghula Khan seems to have
convinced McMahon saheb," he continued, "that
it is the Tibetan authorities who are back of
the disappearance of the C. A. C. C. agents and
of Rankin saheb."

"But—" exclaimed the Tashi Lama. "What
about my visit to Darjeerling?" Ludicrously,
he seemed honestly shocked. "How dare the
sahebs take that Afghan assassin's word against
mine—mine own—eh?"

Rapidly the Depon changed a laugh into a
cough.

"Exactly.   It seems that McMahon saheb fled
from the rain and sat down under the water-
spout; that, failing to trust you, Heaven-Born, he
has trusted Ghula Khan—at least trusted him
enough to investigate—and to utter threats!
Heretofore we had to deal with the C. A. C. C.,
a rich company, but not a company able to make
war.   Now the Raj himself has taken a hand in
the matter.   Heaven-Born!" Kuy-go went on
impressively, "the guns of the Raj are massing
near Darjeeling.   For other news came to the
saheb's ears.   The sahebs have their spies everywhere!   News came from Kashgar and Peking,
from Persia and Nagasaki, from Bokhara and
Moscow!   News—and is it not true news?—
that we, though we claim to be a peaceful nation,

only wishing to be left alone, are accumulating the sinews of war!"

"You mean—" the Tashi Lama was greatly excited—"the sahebs found out about our hidden arsenal, at Chalu?"

"No!"

"Can we do without it?"

"No!"

"Then—what?" asked the Depon.

"It is due before the end of the year!"

"Many things are due—without arriving."

"It *must* come!"

"Must?"

"This is the year of the Wood-Dragon! There is the prophecy!"

"The end of the year is near, Heaven-Born!" said the other. "Just a few days!"

"Time enough, O man of little faith!" thundered the Tashi Lama. "And when that last shipment comes, we will be fully prepared."

"You underestimate the Raj's strength!"

"At least we will be prepared enough to stand the shock of a first attack from the South, to beat them back when they, expecting us to be armed as were our fathers, will charge them with their own devil-devised weapons of destruction! Prepared enough to descend into the Indian plains through the secret passes for a counter-attack! And by that time our friends and allies of the

North and the East will have found an excuse for war—will be ready to come to our aid——"

"I do not altogether trust our friends of the North and the East. They use us as a cat's-paw! Heaven-Born, it has been said that he who introduces himself between Lhassa—and the Dalai Lama himself——"

"The Dalai Lama thinks differently to-day——"

"Because you priests forced his hand! Everything—" argued the Depon stubbornly—"depends upon that first move. And that last arms shipment——"

"Renegade!" stormed the Tashi Lama, his eyes blazing with fury. "Coward! Traitor! Man without faith or honor or manners of decency!" He paused; clapped his hands; sent the monk who ran up for a platoon of soldiers.

"Captain!" he said to their leader as they came. "Arrest this man—the coward, the renegade, the traitor!"

He turned to To Palté:

"We are off for Lhassa! Hurry!"

"And—" asked To Palté—"the Depon?"

"Depon no longer! But the sweeping of the bazar gutter! Discredited! Dishonored! Let him be taken along! The sacred tribunal at Lhassa will decide upon the dog's fate!"

The Depon turned pale. He knew by what

methods of torture—the riding on a spiked saddle, the slow, painful squeezing of thumbs and
ankles, the burning and mutilating—the sacred
tribunal forced confession from those accused of
high treason.   But he did not utter a word.   He
bowed his head stoically on his breast.   Then, as
he passed by Jimmie, he looked up suddenly.
The latter was not quite sure if, just then, all at
once, a fleeting glimmer of recognition had come
into the man's eyes.   Nor did he stop to analyze
why he did what he did.   But—was it merely
sympathy, was it a quick, half-formed thought
that here, perhaps, might be an ally?—at all
events, just as the Depon was being led across
the threshold and while Tashi Lama was making
his final kowtow before the "Pig-faced Goddess,"
Jimmie surreptitiously stuck out his tongue at the
accused man, in sign that here was one who felt
friendly toward him.

A few minutes later they were off again on the
long trek, and it seemed presently that the Tashi
Lama's faith in Tibet's destiny was not misplaced
after all.   For, late that afternoon, as they de-
bouched into the great open plain of central Tibet,
they heard a faint jingling and shouting and, a
few minutes later, steadily increasing, a roaring
and humming, with a jingling of camels' bells, a
thumping of kettle drums, a braying of war
trumpets.

"A caravan from the North!" cried To Palté, spurring his horse alongside the palanquin.

Then a sharp flash of lance points and rifle barrels and metal-bossed shields, a shrill cry spanning the distance: *"Yah! Yah! Hay-n'yang"*; the thunder of galloping horses, the soft, rhymic thud of the dromedaries' padded feet and, a few minutes later, a huge cortège burst into full view, fabulous, glorious in the pink rays of the dying sun.

It was composed of three picked regiments of Lhassa cavalry, several score of Tartar muleteers and camel-riders sitting high on peaked saddles, long lines of batteries being dragged along with the crackle of steel and wood and, finally, hundreds and hundreds of pack animals, ponies and mules and camels, all heavily laden with bales and boxes.

Nor did it need the Tashi Lama's excited whisper: "At last! to convince Jimmie that here was the final arms shipment of which the Depon had spoken and which would mean war in the hills, war in the South, perhaps the clouting of war throughout half Asia.

The leader of the cortege stopped by the Tashi Lama's palanquin. They had a short conversation, winding up with the Tashi Lama's:

"Good, good! By the Buddha!"

Then the two caravans went each on its way,

while the soldiers of both broke into a huge shout
of war that rose to a soul-freezing pitch—a
shout of *"Hay-yai-yai!"*—not a cheer, rousing,
deep-throated, enthusiastic, as European or
American soldiers would give, but a giant heaving
of energy bursting into sound, centering into a
quivering, minor note that dropped like a pall
of death, that, somehow, seemed to partake of
both ocean and hills, of the scarlet day, the night
that came on swift, black wings, and the great,
gold dusted mountains that swept on to Lhassa;
a sound that seemed to bunch all Asia's crunching,
cruel soul into a solid fact.

The arms caravan disappeared south beneath
its fluttering banners in a wavering line of dust;
and not long afterwards the Tashi Lama commanded halt and rest for the night.

"We shall be at Lhassa tomorrow!" he said
to To Palté.   "My people, soldiers and caravanmen, have done well and loyally.   See that extra
rations of food and drink and opium balls are
distributed.   Tomorrow comes the final march."

And so, while the Tashi Lama conferred long
with his lieutenants and with several yellow-
capped abbots who had come down from the
capital, the caravan made camp, squatting about
their cook pots, eating, toasting and smoking the
opium balls, drinking deep of heady rice and
barley wine.

Great joy and excitement pervaded the camp, brushing into Tashi Lama's silken tent. He laughed.

"Listen!" he said, smiling, "It is the right—the spirit of conquerors!"

The tomtoms and gongs thumped without pause. Horns and reed-pipes shrieked and whimpered. Drunken songs stammered forth.

"Let them be merry!" laughed the Tashi Lama. "They have done well!"

And again he turned to the abbots, whispering confidentially, while the riot outside increased a thousandfold, while night dropped completely with its sable cloak, stabbed here and there by the ruby-red ball of a camp fire, while—suddenly—Jimmie made up his mind. He closed his eyes; dropped over backwards with a plop; heard a moment later the Tashi Lama's voice:

"Chandra Das!"

Jimmie sat up again, rubbing his eyes.

"Yes?"

"Tired, eh? Sleepy? Off to bed with you—" the Tashi Lama looked about the tent, shook his head—"you won't be able to sleep here. Go to the palanquin—we'll be talking here for hours. Tomorrow great honor will be yours! You will be permitted to behold the glorious countenance of the *Kyah-gon Rim-po-che,* the Ever Victorious

Lord, the Living Buddha, the Dalai Lama Himself! *Om ma-ni pad-me! Hung!*"

"*Om ma-ni pad-me! Hung!*" mumbled the monks and abbots, twirling their prayer wheels.

"*Om ma-ni pad-me! Hung!*" echoed Jimmy, sharply, sibilantly.

"Hayah!" The Tashi Lama laughed delightedly when he heard, for the first time, the words of the sacred symbol on Jimmie's lips. "At last! Good! Great will be your reward! Now—off with you, and rest well!"

And Jimmie disappeared through the tent flap, his thoughts in a turmoil, a mingling of excitement and nervousness and fear, but uppermost the realization, almost knowledge that, somehow, from him, from him alone, his own young strength and shrewdness, depended a very great destiny.

For the time being he was unwatched, unguarded, free.

Free to do—what?

And how?

CHAPTER XI

ONLY one thing mattered. It was no longer
his duty toward Rankin, his friend. Great
though this duty appeared to Jimmie's loyal
heart, it was now evident to him that it was only
part and parcel of a yet greater duty: the one
he owed to his blood, the one which called to him,
clear and sharp and challenging, in spite of the
fact that he had been born and bred in the Chawkpore bazar slums, that the world of the occident,
America, the world of his ancestors, was no more
to him than a faint racial remembrance. Yet
there was the memory of his father's last words
—it seemed to drop into his soul from the
night-wrapped hills— "You are James Clinton
Weatherby! An American and a gentleman!
And don't you forget it!" And—yes—only one
thing mattered. News of all that had happened,
all that was threatening to happen, must be car-

ried quickly across the border, to the British Raj.

How?

He could not go himself. He was not a mountaineer, did not know the passes, would be apprehended before he had covered a dozen miles.

Rankin? Here the same difficulty obtained. Bennington or one of the other C. A. C. C. agents? And even supposing he succeeded in freeing one of them, and though these three men knew the hills and spoke the language, they were White Men, looked like White Men, would be easily stopped and caught.

There remained only one man. It was the Depon. The latter knew the hills; knew, without doubt, some rapid, secret passes and trails. He seemed to be more tolerant than the other Tibetans, less savage in his racial pride, more inclined to live on terms of peace and amity with the British across the border. Jimmie remembered how the man had argued for peace with the Tashi Lama, had been deposed and taken along as a prisoner, charged with cowardice and high-treason, to be tried by the sacred tribunal at Lhassa. Yes—the Depon had personal reasons, too, urgent personal reasons for being willing, eager, to make his escape, and fear of the tortures in store for him would lend wings to his feet.

It would have to be the Depon. Jimmie said

that he would try and free him.   There was no other way.

He passed through the camp.   It was quite dark, except for the glimmer of the camp fires, dozens of them, strewn like ruby-red flowers over the plain, and bringing occasionally the caravan men and soldiers into sharp relief.   There was still a great uproar, piercing, high-pitched yells of laughter punctuated with the rubbing of tomtoms, the beating of wooden drums, and the blaring of horns; but most of the men had fallen asleep, overcome with food and opium and rice and barley wine, and nobody was sober or wakeful enough to pay attention to Jimmie as, gradually, he edged his way to a little mushroom-shaped tent where the Depon was being kept prisoner.

As Jimmie approached it he saw that here, too, the soldiers had fallen asleep, all but one who was sitting in front of the tent flap, his rifle across his knees.

Jimmie watched him for several minutes from the shadow of a great granite boulder.   He was afraid to the core of his soul.   Then he made up his mind.

He remembered that, amongst his motley and disreputable friends in the Chawkpore bazars, there had been a certain Malak Singh.   The latter had been a very old man, withered, feeble, beady-eyed, tottering.   He had been very poor.

Yet even the wealthier shop-keepers, even occasional, haughty Brahmins passing through the
bazar had treated Malak Singh with respect—respect tinged a little by fear. Jimmie had wondered, had asked questions; and a Hindu of his
acquaintance had told him—whispering the words
in an awed, frightened voice—that, many, many
years ago, Malak Singh had been a Thug, a member of that strange and cruel East Indian caste
that even includes renegade Moslems among its
members, that worships Doorgha, the black-faced,
many-armed goddess of destruction, and that
sacrifices to the blood-lusting deity by killing
travelers in the jungles and on lonely highways,
attacking them in a peculiar way, by using the
roomal, the handerchief of the Thug.

Jimmie and Malak Singh had become great
friends, and often the latter would tell Jimmie
stories of his former prowess and renown
amongst the members of his ghastly caste.

"Ho!" he would say, triumphantly. "Dag-
gers and pistols and clubs are weapons for fools!
In all the world, little brother, there is no weapon
to be compared to our weapon—to the weapon
of the Thugs—to the roomal! Nor is it a question of strength. For even a weaker man can
subdue a stronger—if he know how!"

And one day, when Jimmie had begged him,
he had shown him the trick, in a dark corner of

the bazar, away from the eyes of the police and the curious.

He had taught Jimmie the trick: the hands holding the handkerchief with five inches' space between the thumb joints, the roomal quickly dropped from behind over the victim's head and pressed tightly against the throat, the two thumb joints jerked violently into each side of the wind-pipe. And frequently, in the manner of jest, Jimmie had tried the trick on Mehmet Tugluk and Gandra Pai and the other friends of his youth——

In the manner of a jest!—he thought.

And now it was to be in earnest, grim earnest!

He took out his handkerchief, shivering a little with apprehension of what was to come. But he controlled his nerves.

It would have to be. There was no other way out. He twisted the handkerchief, slowly, care-fully exactly as the old Thug had taught him. Finally it was ready.

He watched for several tense, silent moments. He stared. Then crept forward a little, crouch-ing low in the blotched shadow of a kneeling dromedary that was chewing its cud in the night's peace.

The Tibetan was peering into the night, his head wagging a little from side to side as if he was tired.

Jimmie was quivering with excitement and nervousness. He watched closely. Subconsciously, the soldier must have felt the boy's staring eyes. For, quite suddenly, he turned a little and peered into the depth of shadows where Jimmie was crouching. His eyes, accustomed to the darkness, apparently discovered the hunched form.

He half rose. He seemed undecided what to do, wondering if he should try to rouse his comrades, or jump boldly into the shadows and take his chance.

He hesitated just three seconds too long.

For, with the speed, agility, and silence of a wildcat, Jimmie had slipped around the back of the kneeling dromedary, had flitted to the other side of the tent, had come up behind the soldier, had dropped the tightly stretched roomal over his head. There was no noise, no commotion. Only a sickening little pop. A slight, convulsive writhing. A bending of the man's body backward, his superior strength availing him nothing against the trick of the roomal.

Then Jimmie caught the unconscious, grotesquely flopping body and let it slide on the ground, gently, noiselessly. He looked about warily. Nobody had seen. Quickly he removed the roomal so as not to leave a trace. The man would be stunned and lost to the world for two hours at least; a little more pressure, and he would

have died. Jimmie knew. Malak Singh had
told him.   Too, the roomal left no mark, except
a slight swelling of the throat glands.   The man
would never know what had struck him or how.
He would not be able to explain to his superior
officers, and, ignorant of the Thugs' trick, the
Tibetans would never connect the attack with
Jimmie, would not consider him strong enough to
assault and subdue a grown-up man.

The other soldiers were sleeping and snoring in
drunken stupor.

Jimmie slipped into the tent.   The glow of the
camp fire outside peeked in with a trembling,
crimson wedge, showing the Depon in a corner,
bound hand and foot.

"Hush!" came Jimmie's warning whisper as
the other gave a choked cry, thinking perhaps the
Tashi Lama's hired assassins had come to murder
him without trial.   "Listen!"

He ran up to him, worked feverishly until he
had loosened the bonds, explained in a few, rapid
words, while he squatted by the other's side,
rubbing the numbed arms and legs to restore cir-
culation.

"You will go?" he wound up anxiously.

"Go—I—?" echoed the other.   "And—tell
the Raj—the foreigner?   No, no, no!"

"But—why not?   The sacred tribunal will con-
vict you—torture you—and . . ."

"I know! But—I cannot. This is my own country—I love it!"

"Exactly! It is your own country! You love it! But is not your love strong enough that you will try and save it from disaster, catastrophe, defeat? Remember—the Raj is strong! Offend the Raj—and the Raj will take toll! Come —save your country! Cross the border! Do as I tell you! It is the only way!"

There came a tense pause. The other was silent, thinking, brooding. Finally he inclined his head.

"Yes," he said, dully, sadly, "you are right. It is the only way. I will go."

"Good! But be quick about it," implored Jimmie. "If they catch you—you know—the danger—the torture. . . ."

"Pah!" the other exclaimed contemptuously. "It is not the fear of my own danger—it is not the fear of their tortures which makes me do this thing. It is because I am either a great patriot or——"

"Or——?"

"A black traitor!"

"A great patriot!"

"So I think! But—what will the others think —the Dalai Lama—the Living Buddha——?"

"He, too—I heard you say so—believes in peace——"

"Peace—yes—but with honor! And—shall I be able to—" he slurred, stopped.

Many questions trembled on Jimmie's lips. He wanted to ask the other's advice, about Lhassa, the Dalai Lama, about what he should do and how. But there was no time to be lost. He led the way to the tent flap.

"Hurry!" he said.

"Is it safe outside?"

"Drink and opium have done their work!"

"Thanks be to the Buddha!"

They left the tent, walked through the sleeping camp. Here and there were still singing, carousing men, a drumming of tomtoms and blaring of horns. But nobody paid attention to the two. Near one of the camp fires, where a dozen muleteers were snoring fraternally, the Depon stopped and picked up a bag of provisions.

In back of the palanquin was an acacia grove where the best animals, horses, camels, and mules, were fast asleep. In the semi-darkness, the Depon picked out one of the horses, a blooded, lean, finely bred Marwari mare, soothed her with voice and knowing hands, threw a saddle across her withers, and cinched it tight. He led the horse away, across a bit of rock-strewn heath, jumped into the saddle, and was off.

Jimmie looked after him. Farther on, through a rift in the packed cloud banks, the moon shone brightly.   He saw the trail stretching sharply to the South and Southwest, saw the Depon riding away at a mad gallop, like a Tartar, rising in his stirrups, bent over the horse's neck.   Once the animal reared on end and landed stiffly on its forefeet.   But the Depon, expert horseman, pressed on the curb with full strength, brought his fist down between the horse's ears, and, after a second or two of similar reasoning, the Marwari stretched its splendid, steely body, fell into a long, swinging fox-trot—out into the velvety gloom of the night through the giant shadows of the low, volcanic ridges which flanked the road— out and away.

Jimmie watched for a few seconds.   He heard the disappearing *click-clicketty-click* of the mare's dancing, dainty feet.   Then he returned to the palanquin, slipped in unobserved and, five minutes later, had fallen into dreamless, untroubled sleep.

The next morning there was great excitement in camp when the Depon's disappearance became known.   But, as he had thought, nobody connected Jimmie with it, and there was no further result except a summary court-martial and—Jimmie shuddered a little, felt guilty, but overcame the feeling as he told himself that perhaps, by sacrificing this one man's life he was ultimately saving thousands of others from the grim maws of war—a firing squad, a sharp command: "Fire!"

the thud of a falling body, and a bit of blood caking crimson on the grey ground; and the caravan was off again, while picked, mounted scouts were despatched on the Depon's trail.

Came the last day's march.

First the trail narrowed away from the plain into a stony path over which the caravan, for hours, had to pass in single file, threading in and out amongst gigantic, jagged boulders, and climbing giddy staircases hewn from the living rock of the cliffs while, a few yards below, the Tsango river rushed in a mad, yellow swirl. Everywhere the hillsides were painted with the sacred symbol of the Jewel in the Lotus, in contrasting colors, or carved into sculptures of protecting divinities, most frequent among the latter—very appropriately—being the figure of the *Dolma,* the "Savior-Goddess of the Waters and the Rocks."

On they marched, through the valley of the Kyi, passing through dirty villages where black pigs scurried away at their approach while the inhabitants, fully as dirty as the pigs, lined the roadside, sticking their tongues out in friendly greeting and kowtowing devoutly as the Tashi Lama's palanquin came swinging into sight. On through the Chu'sul defile, and into a fertile stretch of land studded with monasteries, with their priests fattening on the peasants' supersti-

tions, past the tomb of King Ral-pa-chan, greatest
of Tibetan monarchs, and the monument of
Dipankara Srijnana, the Indian Buddhist saint;
and it was early in the afternoon that, zigzagging
up a steep staircase that climbed to a bluff a thousand feet above the green waters of the Kyi, they
caught their first glimpse of the Lhassa suburbs.
Across from the bluff, facing the Holy City, while
down in the valley an incense kiln shot forth a
dense, spiral column of scented smoke up the
mountain side, as a sacrifice to the spirits of the
place.

The caravan halted as if by word of command.
They all descended from their animals and, jaded
and hungry as they were, yet prey to the intense
emotional and religious excitement, they threw
themselves on the ground, while up to the tight,
pigeon-blue skies rose an amazing chant:

"*Om ma-ni pad-me! Hung!*"
"*Om ma-ni pad-me! Hung!*"
"*Om ma-ni pad-me! Hung!*"

Close together they knelt, the many hundreds
of them, the Tashi Lama in the centre, with
curved backs, foreheads and outstretched hands
touching the earth. They swayed rhythmically
from side to side with all the hysterical frenzy of
the Oriental in moments of supreme religious
exaltation; mumbling a great staccato hymn of

guttural, clicky words, with now and then a sharply-defined pause, followed by a deep, heavy murmur.

"Om ma-ni pad-me! Hung!"

And other exclamations, high-pitched, mad, exultant:

"Oh Buddha! This is the sanctuary of thy eternal incarnation—the Jewel in the Lotus! Make it to us a protection from the fires of the great hell Aviki!"

"Oh Buddha! Send us the blessing of thy ten thousand blue lotus field!"

"O Buddha! Open wide the gates of thy mercy that we may pass safely into salvation!"

"O Buddha! How multiform the consolidation of thy world! How marvelous thy understanding!"

And Jimmie, too, felt conscious of a huge excitement as he saw the city stretching at his feet like a flower made of stone petals.

Lhassa—he thought. The Sacred City, the capital of the Forbidden Land!

The holy soil where the living Buddha had ruled for thousands of years—in a land ever undefiled by the foot and hand and rule of the foreigner!

Lhassa!—Asia's last stronghold of mystery and exclusion!

Lhassa—the seat of the gods! The sanctified Rome of Central Asia!

Here, as the caravan descended the farther side of the bluff, it came more and more fully into view, from behind a curtain of rock spanning the two bold guardian hills of the town, that of the Potola and that of the Iron Mountain, pierced in its centre by the western gate, the Pargo Ka-ling, the "Middle-Door Barrier."

A fascinating town it seemed, with crooked streets and alleys, with substantial, three-storey stone houses carefully white-washed, the beams picked out in blazing colors, with its wealth of temples and monasteries, their fascades emblazoned with great purple and gold monograms of the mystic *Om ma-ni* legend, with its cool gardens of flowering trees, with its motley populace thronging the roads; travel-stained, ruddy-cheeked, stalwart nomads from Outer Mongolia, and the Siberian steppes, dressed in yellow felt suits and greasy sheepskins, riding ponies, and their strangely fair-complexioned women, covered with barbaric silver oranments, and riding astride like their husbands, helping the latter in the herding of their double-humped Bactrian dromedaries and their pack-ponies; shiny-pated monks, ruby-robed, yellow-capped or red-capped, twirling their prayer-wheels; townspeople in homespun, townspeople in yellow duffel, townspeople in rich silks and furs; supercilious-looking Chinese, dressed in the eternal blue of China and looking contemptuously upon the Tibetans whom they consider to be savages; half-breed kokos of mixed Chinese and Tibetan blood; swarthy, Jewish-looking Tartars from Ladak and Kashmir; squat, smiling Nepalese crowned with porkpie-caps; free-walking, gigantic Kham mountaineers; round-headed, beady-eyed Kalmuks from Russia; all haggling, laughing, chatting, well disciplined by the *Korchak,* the native Tibetan police.

On passed the caravan, past the *Jo-kang,* the "House of the Master," Lhassa's chief temple, past the *Chomo-ling* and the *Tengye-ling,* the two royal monasteries, past the Dragon Temple with its enameled roof flashing like the shooting of a million dragon-flies, on through the sacred Circular Road, across the *Yutok,* the "Turquoise-tiled Bridge," and up to the "Square of the Wild Asses" where the caravan came to a halt.

A town strong and beautiful and fascinating and mysterious, and, in the distance, overtowering the whole, rose a gigantic palace built out of the granite hillside, soaring up in even tiers, curving inward like a great stony bay dammed by the sweep of the crenellated, winglike battlements, descending into the dip of the valley with an avalanche of bold masonry.

"The Potala!" said the Tashi Lama, pointing at the palace. "The home of the Dalai Lama!"

CHAPTER XII

JIMMIE stared. The sheer, majestic beauty
of the place took his breath away. Different
it was from the tawdry, overornate Hindu archi-
tecture to which he was used.

As he looked more closely he saw that it was
not a single edifice, but a mass of lofty buildings
that covered the hillside, that dominated the entire town, but most glorious of all the central
cluster of buildings, with its five gilt pavilions,
and of a dull crimson color that gives to it it's
name of Potala, the "Red Palace," and the entire
central portion draped with long curtains of dark
purple yak-hair tapestries hanging from the windows. A fascinating pile it was, flashing high
and colorful above the surrounding woods and
hills, well destined to strike awe and veneration
into the hearts of the Buddhist pilgrims from all

Asia who cross to the Holy City through the barren uplands; yet a place, too, stout for defence, with the northern side protected by the hill's precipitous crag, a loopholed wall framing the other three sides—defence built perhaps in memory of the marauding Jungarian Tartars who, twenty thousand strong, mounted on swift dromedaries, and under the leadership of Prince Tee Wang Rabadn Tamerlani, swept down from the plains of Turkestan early in the Eighteenth Century, crossed the desert, conquered and sacked Lhassa, and ruled the Forbidden Land until driven out by a Chinese army sent from Shensi.

The Tashi Lama smiled at Jimmie's enthusiasm.

"Ah—" he said, with gentle irony, "can it indeed be that my barbaric race and its worthless accomplishments are finding favor in your eyes, my Chandra Das? Can it be that you, although born and bred in a land dominated by the all-knowing all-understanding White sahebs, are yet Asian enough to admire the hideous endeavor of us outer savages? Hayah—you shall see more of it!"

He turned to To Palté, giving quick instructions for the disbanding and quartering of the caravan.

"Have the sahebs taken to the Na-chung

monastery," he added.   "Then follow me and
Chandra Das to the Potala."

So Rankin and the three C. A. C. C. agents
were taken to the Na-chung monastery, below
Potala, below Potala Hill, which is the home of
the chief soothsayer of Tibet who is supposed to
be an incarnation of the *Pe-kar,* the great Mongolian King of the Demons, and addressed by the
length and sonorous title of "The exalted foot-
stool, composed of the corpses of the infidels, on
which rest the feet of the Defender of the Faith,
the chief incarnation of the Almighty Conqueror
of the Enemies of the Three Worlds, the Golden
Lamp of Sublime Wisdom!"

In the meantime, advancing in gorgeous procession, preceded and followed by a retinue of
chanting priests and monks, the Tashi Lama
moved up toward Potala Hill, with Jimmie by his
side.

As the procession passed, the crowds of men
and women who lined the streets kowtowed
deeply.   Here the houses were nearly all one-
storeyed, after the Chinese manner, with neat
turf walls in front enclosing little flower gardens
with pots of blooming asters, marigolds, stocks
and hollyhocks, and with nasturtiums enlivening
the window sills.   But the streets themselves were
in a revoltingly dirty condition, littered over with

all sorts of refuse and miry sewage in which scores of lean, unwholesome-looking pigs wallowed and grunted repulsively.

Nearing the Potala Hill, they passed the residence of the *amban,* the Chinese governor. It was typically Pekinese. For before the doorway, with its painted dragons and its blue-robed, pig-tailed watchmen, stood an immense, bronze incense burner flanked by tall poles from which the imperial dragon flag floated in the cool breeze, and two immense masts with a dovecot-like frame work that held great crimson and violet paper lanterns.

Jimmie knew presently that the Lhassa runners who had joined the caravan on the way to return to the capital, had spread the news of his coming broadcast. For, here and there, as they passed kowtowing abbots, red-capped and yellow-capped, he heard their gliding murmurs, as they pointed surreptitious fingers at him, that he was the "Conciliatory sending from a foreign land," mentioned in the ancient prophecy as coming near the end of the Wood-Dragon, the "youth to give a true and shining nimbus to the Jewel in the Lotus, and to bring victory!" And he grinned with mocking, boyish enjoyment as a wrinkled old monk kissed the hem of his tunic with a deep-throated *"Om ma-ni!"*, as he thought what his old friends in the Chawkpore bazar, Mehmet Tugluk the

The Red Palace towering above them

Afghan and Gandra Rai the Hindu, would say if they could see him now.

Up a steep staircase of several hundred steps they zigzagged, the Red Palace towering threateningly above them. Half way up they rested for a few minutes on the circular bastion, the so-called "Horse Stage," then went on, finally passing through a gate into the outer courtyard, through another courtyard, crammed with human life, up a broad flight of stairs, and into another courtyard, where a hundred yellow-robed priests were awaiting them, swinging golden incense-burners.

They came to a massive, silver-studded door. One of the abbots drew a foot-long, skewer-like key from his girdle, and opened it.

Then entered. The door closed behind them. And as he heard the click of the lock, the little metallic click of finality which seemed to shut out the outer world, as he heard the Tashi Lama's words: "The home of the Dalai Lama, the Living Buddha, the Jewel in the Lotus!", again a certain superstitious sensation rushed upon Jimmie, a clay-cold, shivering sensation that took possession of his body and soul—something partaking neither of the spiritual nor the physical, yet at the same moment akin to both—something that was beyond the power of analysis, of guessing, of fear even.

But he controlled himself with an effort.   He
followed while the priests led the way through
many suites of rooms supported by double rows
of pillars whose capitals were shaped into pendant
lotus forms, sometimes crowned with fantastic
lateral struts carved into the likenesses of horsemen or war chariots, past balconies which clung
like birds' nests to the sheer side of the palace,
through doors of inlaid ivory, others crusted with
looking-glass, still others with polished jade and
chrysoprase.   There was furniture of all ages,
from all the Asian lands, Chinese and Tibetan
and Hindu and Tartar, Mongol and Arab and
Bokharan.   On through fair gardens hanging on
the side of the hills, and again through long suites
of rooms, and up and down steep stairs encoun-
tering hundreds of yellow-robed and red-robed
priests who all bowed low, murmuring greetings,
sticking out their tongues.

They came out into a corridor, hewn evidently from the living rock of Potala Hill.
There the Tashi Lama stopped.

"The Jewel in the Lotus is waiting for me," he
said.   "I shall send for you when I need you
—perhaps tomorrow—perhaps the next day,
Chandra Das. Here—" to a tall, ruddy-
complexioned man.   "Ung Changren!"

"Heaven-born!"

"See to it that our friend Chandra Das is well

taken care of. And—" to Jimmie—"is there, belike, any message which you would like to send through me to the Jewel in the Lotus?"

Jimmie considered in silence for several seconds while the Tashi Lama waited anxiously. Then he smiled to himself. After all, came his shrewd thought as he remembered what he had heard from Bennington as well as from the Depon as to the Dalai Lama not having always been in sympathy with the party which advocated war and strife, he was telling no more than the truth.

"Yes," he replied slowly. "There is indeed a message which I would like to send———"

"Ah!" the Tashi Lama sucked in his breath.

"A message of my devotion and friendship and . . ."

"Your willingness to help us?" cut in the Tashi Lama, rapidly, significantly.

"Indeed!"

The other raised his hands.

"Thanks be to the Excellent Lord Gautama Buddha, the Perfectly Awakened One!" he exclaimed sonorously.

And he went on his way, to the right, while Ung Changren led Jimmie to the left, for many minutes, through that fantastic blending of granite hill and bastioned palace which is the Potala, through rooms and rooms and again rooms, up and down, some of the apartments ablaze with raw, clashing colors, others in dull somber shades which melted into each other. Several times they stopped for rest, and in many of the rooms, or patrolling the corridors on noiseless, padded slippers, they encountered palace officials, clad in rainbow silks, who stepped aside and salaamed with outstretched hands.

On, through gloomy, cave-like landings!

"The heart of the hill!" explained the monk. "For this palace covers acres and acres. Nobody knows how large it is. Not even the Jewel in the Lotus himself. It is impossible to say where the hill begins and where the man-fashioned palace ends. We are walking only in one direction. But over there—" he pointed to the right where other corridors were jutting away crookedly— "over there are more passages and rooms which connect with the Taragarh, the giant fortress that flanks the southern bastions."

He opened a door.

"We have arrived," he said. He indicated a large room, luxuriously furnished in the Chinese manner. "Rest yourself, Chandra Das. I shall return presently. And—" with a kindly smile— "are you ready for food?"

"Yes!" Jimmie smiled back at him, with immediate, sympathetic liking for the ruddy-skinned monk.

"Good!   A dish of curried rice perhaps, since you are a Hindu?   Ho!" he laughed.   "I would not trust you very far with a dish of curried rice, my little Hindu!"   And he added, in gliding Hindu: *"Gidar rakhe mana ke thati*—it is not wise to keep meat on trust with a jackal!"

"Oh—" Jimmie was startled.   "You speak Hindu?"

"Yes.   I am a Buddhist from your side of the border, living in Kashmir many years, until—" he bowed, twirled his prayer-wheel devoutly, "faith came to me—the Buddha spoke to me in the night—and I came here, to worship the Jewel in the Lotus—to seek peace!   Peace!" he echoed, with a deep, morose sigh, and he left the room while Jimmie stared after him, glad, somehow, of the knowledge that this man, too, was a native of Hindustan.

Food came.   Jimmie ate.   Evening dropped, and a servant entered and lit the lamps.

Jimmie stepped out on the balcony which jutted from the room.   It gave on the inner courtyard. He looked out.

The inrushing night lay thick about while a deep, massive silence like that of a distant sea ebbed and flowed and whirled and eddied in regular beats, spreading far out and beyond into the city of Lhassa.   The palace, a warren of teeming humanity, and humanity's wives and children and mothers-in-law and visiting cousins, was preparing to retire for the night. Grooms and grass-cutters, camel-drivers and clerks, paunchy employees of the Dalai Lama's treasury, villagers from the countryside come to present a petition or to call on friend or relative, desert men who had brought the slim taxes of the farther lands, sellers of shawls and perfumes, of Chinese embroideries and Persian brocades and gold-threaded Kashmir muslin, priests and monks and fighting-men—one by one they passed through the inner gate.

Finally the whole place was deserted, and there was no noise, except the creaking sound of a sentinel grounding his long, black bamboo lance or the click-clack-click of a metal scabbard tip being dragged against the stone pavement as the officers of the night watch made the rounds of the bastions.

A great, overwhelming feeling of loneliness rushed upon Jimmie. He turned, startled, as he felt a hand on his shoulder, and heard a voice:

"Look!"

It was Ung Changren speaking. He had come silently out on the balcony.

"Beyond! Look beyond!" he repeated, pointing to the West, away from the Potala, where the streets of the city and the boxwood hedges of the gardens ran together in a single sheet of purplish black, above them the dim white of the roof tops.

Jimmie looked. To the west a chain of huge hills soared to the heavens in great tiers. For leagues, quite clear against the eternal snow fields of the higher peaks which flushed sharp under the brilliant, silvery rays of the rising moon, pine and beech woods rose over the enormous, steep slopes. In the very far distance, beneath the sun's crimson afterglow, the roof of a temple burned like the plumage of a gigantic peacock.

"A peaceful land, eh?" came the monk's low voice. He stopped; then continued as if talking to himself: "A most blessed land! A land dear to the Buddha's heart!" And, staring straight at Jimmie: "And you—don't you think so, Chandra Das?"

"Yes!" came Jimmie's sincere reply.

"Ah—?" The monk seemed astonished. "You do?"

"Indeed!"

"Then, thinking as you do, why disturb the white peace of this land with crimson, slashing ambition? Why give the swish and thrust of the sword when only fair words are needed? Why make for the shock of armed men when—Ah!" Suddenly the man was silent. He turned an ashen grey. "No, no, no!" he went on, as if frightened by something in his own words, some great and hidden danger. "Forget my words,

Chandra Das! I, too, am from Hindustan—please, please—do not give me away! Forget my rash and foolish words!" He seemed torn by a very agony of fear. "I did not mean what I said! I—" pitifully—"I was only jesting, belike! You—you are the friend of the Tashi Lama—the youth of whom the prophecy speaks! Please, please—do not give me away, little brother!"

He bowed, ran from the balcony, out of the room, still protesting that he had only jested, while Jimmie looked after him, puzzled, wondering, speculating. Then all at once, he said to himself that he understood. Why, he thought, there was talk of two parties at Lhassa, and Ung Changren, judging from his words, seemed to belong to the other party, the minority, which had been for peace with the Raj until, as far as Jimmie could make out, the Dalai Lama had been persuaded otherwise or overruled by the fighting monks. Ung Changren, looking over the peaceful town, had given way to a sudden impulse, a sudden great emotion, and had spoken out the hidden despair in his heart. Then, as suddenly, realization had come to him that this Chandra Das was the youth of the prophecies, and that he must of necessity be a friend of the Tashi Lama, an upholder of the latter's militant policies.

Here then, in the ruddy-complexioned monk

from Kashmir, was a friend, thought Jimmie; and, feeling less lonely, less despondent, he went to bed.

Only one thing bothered him: a question of time.   How long, he wondered, would it take the Depon, always supposing he was not caught, to reach and cross the border and to communicate with Sir Hector McMahon, the British-Indian commander-in-chief?   Ten days?   Two weeks? Or, perhaps, less since he was doubtless familiar with some of the quick, secret trails and passes? But the end of the year, the lucky year of the Wood-Dragon, was drawing to a close.   The fighting priests would make up their minds, doubly encouraged now that the great arms shipment had come out of the Mongolian plains; would finally force the Dalai Lama's hand.   Yet, Jimmie figured, the Depon was sure to overtake the caravan, and a number of weeks would elapse before the arms shipment had reached the Chalu armory, before the weapons and ammunition had been distributed, the troops fully mobilized, not to forget all the other preparations for actual war.

Yes, he thought, time was still on his side.   But how should he use this element of time?   What would he do?   What could he do?   There was the Dalai Lama, the great, unknown, mysterious quantity.   In him alone rested the final decision, the solution of the whole question.   He would have to speak to him, alone, in private, when he was uninfluenced by the leaky-tongued, bullying priests and abbots, the shrewd Tashi Lama, To Palté, and the others; and—again Jimmie felt very young and very lonely—who was he, a youth just on the edge of manhood, born and bred in the slums of Chawkpore, to talk to the descendant of the gods, to the Living Buddha—to argue with the Jewel in the Lotus?

"Got to try it—that's all!" he said to himself, sturdily, as finally he fell asleep.

CHAPTER XIII

THE next day passed, a second, a third. There was no word from the Tashi Lama. Nor did Ung Changren return.

Three times a day a servant came with trays of food. He showed Jimmie a tiny garden, clinging to the side of the hill, no bigger than six square feet, and reached by a secret door.

"If you want fresh air," he said laconically.

Jimmie tried to draw him into conversation, but did not succeed.

There was never a word from the Tashi Lama, never a sign. Not that, otherwise, the hours did not have their quota of interest and excitement. For there was a continuous going and coming, down in the courtyard, of hurrying messengers, a great beating of tomtoms and gongs. Twice, watching from the balcony, he saw Rankin and the three C. A. C. C. agents led into the palace under heavy guard and led out again later on; and late one night, as he was going to bed, from a room which seemed to be directly underneath his own, drifted up a great turmoil, a chanting and singing of many voices, finally peaking into an amazing, staccato hymn:

> *"The tawny lamps of war are lit!*
> *The bitter cry of war is in the market place!*
> *The clank of war is in the high hills!*
> *Hail—Jewel in the Lotus—Hail!"*

Then a sudden pause; a voice—Jimmie recognized it as the Tashi Lama's— "Soon, brothers, soon! Cometh soon the final prophecy of fulfillment, the prophecy of the year of the Wood-Dragon!"—then silence.

On the next day Jimmie made up his mind. He turned to the servant who had come in with breakfast.

"I want to talk to the Tashi Lama," he said.

The servant bowed deeply.

"Word will doubtless be sent you at the proper time, Chandra Das," he answered.

"Yes—but I am getting a little tired waiting. I want to see the Tashi Lama soon. Tell him so!"

"Oh—" the other was profoundly shocked. "Who am I, the very small and worthless one, to

bring such a message to him who is almost a God?
Consider, Chandra Das!"

"All right!" Jimmie hid a smile.   "But there's
one thing you *can* do!"

"Yes?"

"I want to stretch my legs.   I want to go for
a walk."

"There is the garden," suggested the servant.

"Too small!   And I know every stick and
stone of it, every last leaf and flower and blade
of grass."

"Very well.   I shall report to my superiors
and see what can be done."

The servant bowed and withdrew.

Evidently he succeeded.   For that afternoon
Ung Changren came into the room and took Jimmie downstairs to a great park, and walked by
his side.

But the monk was morose, apathetic.   He
hardly opened his mouth the whole time.   He
was evidently frightened to the core of his soul.

The same thing happened the next day: the
same walk, the same park, the same frightened,
silent monk; and, on the third day, Jimmie, perhaps giving way to his inherited American impatience, decided suddenly to take the bull by the
horns.

"Ung Changren," he said, "the other time—
when you spoke about peace——"

"No, no!" the monk interrupted, kowtowing. "I was jesting—forget my words——"

"You were not jesting!"

"Yes, yes—I was!"

"No, no—you were not!" laughed Jimmie. "And I shall not forget——"

"But——"

"You see—I happen to agree with you."

"You—what?"

"That's it! I believe in peace myself. That is exactly the reason why I am here." In spite of his nervousness and anxiety, Jimmie was enjoying himself hugely. For, born and bred in the Chawkpore slums, he liked intrigues and, where the latter were concerned, was of a precocious shrewdness which an American politician might have envied him.

"But—" stammered Ung Changren, "the Tashi Lama——"

"What about him?"

"Aren't you the youth of whom the prophecy speaks—who will come from a foreign land to help——?"

"So I have been told. But I am all for peace just the same. Really!" insisted Jimmie.

"Oh——"

Ung Changren looked up, suspicious of a trap. Then something in Jimmie's eyes showed him that the latter was sincere, and he burst into a full-toned chanting of thanks:

"Praised be the Buddha, the Perfectly Awakened One!"

Over and over he repeated it, until Jimmie interrupted him with:

"Praise the Buddha afterwards, when the whole thing is settled.   But let's settle it first——"

"What?"

"Peace, Ung Changren!"

"But—how?"

"That's just what is bothering me, too.   Come —let's stroll up and down and appear less excited. There may be people watching us.   You know what the Hindus say: No use letting a bird fly away, and then run after it!"

So they walked amongst the trees, talking in an undertone, Jimmie asking questions and the monk replying.

"Look here," said the former finally.   "Let me go over what you told me.   You say that the peace party is in the minority, that the Dalai Lama is really with you, but that he will not go against the oracles and prophecies?"

"Yes."

"Furthermore—" the boy went on—"you told me that, though your party is numerically weak, you have certain weapons?"

"Yes," replied the monk proudly, "numbers are not everything!   A well cannot be filled with dew drops!"

"What weapons?"

"We have a much quicker and better system of espionage than the Tashi Lama's party."

"For instance?" insisted Jimmie.

"Our system of communicating through the hills—of sending messages—words—warnings—information——"

"Yes?"

"We know how to send word, by runner, through secret trails, by drum code and smoke signals, much quicker than the others."

"How much quicker, Ung Changren?"

"Perhaps two or three days—between Lhassa and the border."

"And the other party does not suspect?" asked Jimmie, all his artful bazar training coming to the surface.

"They have no idea!   The dream of the cat is all about mice—not about other cats!"

"Good!   Now—you know the Depon?"

"Yes."

"Good again.   Listen—" Jimmie told him about how he had helped the Depon to escape; added; "he belongs to your party?"

"He had to obey—as we all have to obey.   But he is for peace."

"But—he knows your system of sending messages?

"He can communicate with your confidential agents here and there?"

"Yes," replied the monk.

"So that, if he succeeds and warns the Raj, you will know about it a couple of days before the Tashi Lama?"

"Doubtless! But, even if the Depon succeeds, the Tashi Lama's party will insist on war!"

"Wait a moment," cut in Jimmie, more and more enjoying the coiling intrigue. "You spoke of the strength of prophecies, didn't you?"

"Yes."

"Very well. Here is where you can help. Would you mind letting me know just as soon as, through your own quick system, you hear from the Depon?"

"Why?"

Jimmie laughed.

"Remember the prophecy of the Wood-Dragon!" was all the explanation he would vouchsafe. "You will let me know, won't you?"

"Yes."

"Another question. How sincere is the Tashi Lama?"

"In his belief in war?" asked the monk.

"No. In his belief in prophecies. You, after all, are Indian-born—you are not a Tibetan——"

"I understand what you mean," replied Ung Changren. "We of the South are more—ah— enlightened. But the Tashi Lama is Tibetan. He believes in oracles and prophecies and the many superstitions as I believe in the salvation of the blessed Lord Buddha."

"Good!"

The next day, shortly after the noon hour, the Tashi Lama entered Jimmie's room.

"Come with me!" he said. "The Jewel in the Lotus will give you audience. Great honor will be yours. And remember your promise———"

"What promise?"

The Tashi Lama smiled.

"Not to tell the cat what you can tell the ti-ger! Not to take silver when you can get gold! To tell the Dalai Lama if, belike, you found out one or two interesting bits of information amongst the sahebs—eh?"

Jimmie thought; then, suddenly, he made up his mind. "Think—think well—then do—at once!" had been his dying father's advice. He remembered it now.

"I cannot speak about it—yet!" he said, care-fully watching the other, recalling what the monk had told him about the man's superstitious na-ture, yet wondering how far he might go. "I— I have not yet been allowed———"

"Allowed to do what?"

Again Jimmie paused and thought; there had been a fakir, a sainted mendicant, of his boyhood acquaintance in the Chawkpore bazars. He remembered how that unwashed worthy had played on the credulity of the simple country folk by impromptu, semi-religious oracles, greatly to the amusement of the sharp-witted town boys.

"There are the voices—" he said slowly.

"What voices?"

"The voices which speak to me in the night—with tongues of prophecy and promise of fulfillment—the voice of the Wood-Dragon. . . ."

"Ah—" the Tashi Lama breathed deeply. He clicked his prayer-wheel. "It is right! It is true! First permission must be granted by the gods!"

"Yes," replied Jimmie, not knowing what else he should say.

"The Buddha grant that permission be given you soon. For time presses. I myself shall pray long tonight in the temple of the Precious Enthroned! I myself shall implore the Perfectly Awakened One to give you permission! Come now! Bow your knee before the Jewel in the Lotus!"

They stepped out into the corridor, and crossed a number of rooms, up and down stairs, coming into a huge hall, over a hundred feet high, at the western end of which stood the colossal mausoleum called "The Ornament of the World," which enshrines the bodily relics of the first Dalai Lama; a beautiful shrine richly adorned with gold and precious stones, while the steps of its plinths are used for countless ages for the votive offerings of Buddhist princes and chiefs on pilgrimage to Lhassa.

Here they were joined by a procession of shaven-headed young priests, in claret-colored robes, swinging incense-burners, beating drums, clashing cymbals, and blaring thin-shanked horns, while a head-priest walked in front of them, chanting loudly:

"There has arisen the illuminator of the World! The Protector of the World! The Maker of Light who gives eyes to the world, which is blind, to cast away its burden of sin! Buddha is without sin! He is out of the miry pit! He stands on dry ground!"

"Hail—Jewel in the Lotus—Hail!" chanted the priests.

Near the farther end of the hall they stopped, bowed, and receded a few steps while the Tashi Lama, motioning to Jimmie to follow him, opened a door.

They entered. The room in which they found themselves was small and empty.

Jimmie looked about.

It was furnished in ancient, severe Chinese

style, the walls being covered with Kienlung silks
of dark blue embroidered with black and silver
dragons, a thick-napped, brown Tibetan rug on
the floor, a few teakwood chairs, and in the
centre, about three feet from the ground, a simple dais with a seat of five purple cushions,
stamped with the mystic symbol.   On a small
table near the dais stood a tiny vase holding wild-
flowers and a jade drinking-cup, and there was no
other furniture except a large, stationary prayer-
wheel.

A few seconds later a further door opened.
Two priests entered, chanting a hymn:

"To Thee who art clean and pure from all
taint of sin, and celebrated in the three worlds!
Reverence be to Thee!

"Saint!   Whose heart is at rest and who de-
lightest to explain the doubts and perplexities of
men!   Thy aim is pure!   Thy blood is the salvation of men!   Thy practices are perfect!   Reverence be to Thee!

"Teacher of the four truths and the seven
truths who rejoiceth in salvation!   Who being
Thyself free from sin desireth to free the world
from sin with the sacrifice of thy blood!   Reverence be to Thee!"

The priests took up their positions to the left
and right of the door, and a second later another
man came in quickly, noiselessly, on padded slip-

pers. The Tashi Lama threw himself on the ground, rapidly whispering to Jimmie to do likewise.

The latter obeyed.

Glancing up surreptitiously, hearing the Tashi Lama's sibilant words: "The Jewel in the Lotus!", he felt momentarily just a little disappointed, just a little disillusioned, when he realized that this small, thin man who had come in, who was taking a seat cross-legged on the dais, was the Dalai Lama, the Living Buddha, the spiritual overlord of millions of people throughout China and Russia and Siberia, Central Asia, Mongolia, and Northern India, who consider the very murmuring of his name a meritorious action equivalent to a thousand prayers.

To see Lhassa—to see the Dalai Lama himself! These had been Jimmie's dreams ever since he had listened to the tales of Tibetan traders in the Chawkpore bazar. Here was the moment of which he had dreamed—and he felt a chilly reaction. He was not sure himself what he had expected to find. Perhaps some eight-foot gold-colored giant bedecked with jewels and barbarous witch-charms. What he did see was a middle-aged, lean man dressed in a simple robe of dark red wool without ornaments of any sort; and the face above the robe was calm, passionless, clean-shaven, with thin, ascetic lips, a high-bridged nose, prominent cheekbones, and deep, narrow-lidded eyes.

A patient face it was; patient and kindly and rather wearied; and, as his feeling of disappointment disappeared, Jimmie became conscious of a curious sympathy, an honest, human liking for this man. Hardly realizing what he was doing, he looked up; he smiled instinctively and the Dalai Lama returned the smile.

"Rise, my friends," he said, with a wave of an emaciated hand.

They   obeyed.   The   Tashi   Lama   bowed deeply.

"This is the boy of whom I told you, Holiness," he said. "Chandra Das, the youth from a foreign land—the conciliatory sending who is mentioned in the prophecy of the Wood-Dragon——"

"Yes, yes, yes—" the Dalai Lama's voice was flat and weary. "The prophecy!" He paused, thought. "Tell me, Tashi Lama, there is no doubt about the prophecy?"

"No doubt, Holiness! I made sure of it. I consulted the many oracles as you commanded; here, and at Gyantse, as well as the oracle of Saint Padma Atisha's oracle at Ne-t'ang. They all agree."

"Ah?"

"They shall speak about the year of the Wood-

Dragon being the lucky year to bring happiness
to the land and the faith. They all speak about
the sending from a foreign land which shall give
the final word—the final peace——"

"Peace! Yes——"

"Peace through war, Holiness! The sahebs'
peace! All the way from Chalu, after I fell in
with Chandra Das, after I read in the almanac
confirmation of this being the lucky year, after
I interpreted the prophecy of the Wood-Dragon,
I talked with abbots and monks, saintly men,
well versed in the scriptures. I consulted all the
oracles—all! Holiness! There is no doubt of
it! Peace—through war!"

"Aye!" said the Dalai Lama. "So the messages have been interpreted. And yet—" He
shrugged his shoulders, interrupted himself; then
he turned to Jimmie, speaking in a direct and
kindly manner! "I understand from the Tashi
Lama that you lived among the sahebs, gaining
their confidence, and that there you learned certain things of importance of which you wished to
speak to me—to me alone?"

"Yes." Momentarily Jimmie felt strangely
tongue-tied. He did not want to lie to this man.
He liked him. "But—I—" he slurred, stopped.

It was the Tashi Lama who came to his rescue.
He took a step forward.

"Holiness," he said. "Certain voices speak to

Chandra Das in the night. When the voices give permission, he will tell you."

"Very well." The Dalai Lama rose. "The audience is ended. I shall make my final decision after the voices have spoken, giving permission."

He stepped from the dais and left the room, while again the Tashi Lama and Jimmie prostrated themselves on the ground, while again the priests chanted in a minor key:

"Protector of the world! Reverence be to Thee!

"By Thy appearance all the mansions of distress shall be swept empty and clean!

"Hail—Jewel in the Lotus—Hail!"

CHAPTER XIV

DAYS came, tense, hushed, pinched in between the greenish sheen of the strong Northern sun and the lavender outlines of the farther hills; days rising and waning to the eternal chanting of the priests; nervous, expectant days, while the Tashi Lama, now a frequent visitor to Jimmie's room, waited for the voices which would grant the latter permission to speak and fulfil the ancient prophecy, while Jimmie waited for word from the Depon to reach him through Ung Changren's lips. Two weeks had elapsed. Jimmie said to himself; by this time, if he had escaped, the Depon must have crossed the border and communicated with the Raj; the year of the Wood-Dragon was nearly over—and then the final casting of the dice of fortune.

If only the Depon would send word!—was Jimmie's daily prayer. For he had thought out everything constructively, minutely, in detail, using every last ounce of his cool American common sense, every last ounce of his bazar-bred shrewdness. He had rehearsed the scene that was to come over and over again until he knew every word and gesture by heart. If only the Depon would send word!

And so another day came and passed into memory; another evening; another night.

"The last day of the year is tomorrow!" the Tashi Lama had said. "May the Buddha grant you permission to speak, Chandra Das!"

Jimmie echoed the prayer in his heart.

All that night excitement brushed through the Potala like a massive wave. All night the drums beat and droned. All night a savage muttering drifted up from the courtyard. All night the horns brayed, the cymbals clashed, the incense swirled in perfumed streamers. All night the gongs and tomtoms tolled, dully, portentously, and with an insufferable minor cadence.

Jimmie could not sleep. He felt morose, unhappy, afraid.

It was towards morning that he heard the door opening. He looked up, startled.

"I—it is I!" came Ung Changren's voice as he flitted ghost-like into the room.

"News?"

"Yes. The Depon has reached safety, has sent a message. But it was delayed."

"Tell me—quick!"

"He has convinced McMahon saheb that Tibet means trouble. The Raj acted, immediately, sharply. The Raj's guns are starting from Darjeeling. The Raj has made representations to the powers in North and East Asia, threatening them with his warships, with the wrath of the other saheb countries. The Raj caught the North and the East unprepared, has forced guarantees of neutrality from them."

Jimmie did not understand all these political details; but he did understand when the monk continued that, single-handed, without help from its allies in the rest of Asia, Tibet could not fight the British, that the latter would no longer believe Tibetan promises and fair words, but would invade the land immediately, without a declaration of war, unless the Dalai Lama himself took charge of the negotiations and sued for peace.

"And—" Ung Changren added—"it is too late for that. The monks are drunk with superstitions, with the lust of power and blood and glory and conquest; they will not permit the Dalai Lama to draw back. All the prophecies point their way—all——"

"All but one!" smiled Jimmie. "Didn't you say the Depon's message was delayed?"

"Yes. Somewhere in the hills. The message should have been here the day before yesterday. And now—why—in a few hours the Tashi Lama, too, will have received word that the Raj has found out about the Tibetan intrigues."

"Won't that cause him to reconsider—to make a bid for peace?"

"On the contrary! He will draw the sword of audacity and throw away the scabbard of pre-caution! Hayah! He will strike quickly, hop-ing that by his own surprise attack he may coun-teract the Raj's! There *are* the prophecies— they all point their way. . . ."

"All but one," replied Jimmie. "There is yet a certain hope."

Ung Changren left, and, shortly afterwards, Jimmie opened the door and called loudly for the servant. The latter came, sleepily rubbing his eyes.

"Yes, Chandra Das?" he asked.

"I wish to see the Tashi Lama! At once!"

"Oh!" the servant expostulated. "Impos-sible!"

"I must—I tell you!"

"And I tell you that it is impossible—quite out of the question, Chandra Das!"

"Why so?"

"The great war council is assembled in the Outer Hall of the Gods. Today is the last day

of the year of the Wood-Dragon.   The Tashi
Lama is attending the Jewel in the Lotus."

"Call him just the same!"

"I would not dare, Chandra Das.   They
would put my head at my feet."

"No, no! On the contrary.   You will receive a great and shining reward.   Go to the
Tashi Lama.   Tell him the Buddha spoke to me
in the night.   I swear to you—no harm will
come to you!"

The servant was off on a run and, fifteen minutes later, the Tashi Lama rushed into Jimmie's
room.

"It is true what the servant told me?" he asked,
feverishly.

"Yes.   Voices spoke to me.   A prophecy—a
message—a warning——"

"Tell me!"

"I must see the Jewel in the Lotus—to him
alone can I tell the prophecy and the warning——"

"Impossible!   He is giving most important
audience!"

"I must see him!   Now!   No time is to be
lost!" implored Jimmie, remembering what Ung
Changren had told him, that within a few hours
the Tashi Lama, too, would have messages from
the Indian border.

"Very well.   Come with me!"

A few minutes later Jimmie found himself in the "Outer Hall of the Gods," the huge throne room, surrounded by colonnades of crimson pillars that supported elaborately carved beams, with a paneled ceiling studded with brilliant mosaics of precious stones, while the walls were covered with jade and with miniatures painted on gold and ivory.

The place was packed with abbots and monks and priests and officers. Intense excitement prevailed. On all sides was a savage humming that rose at times to frenzied yells and that drowned the thumping of the drums and the loud braying of the war trumpets. At the farther end, on a high dais, the Dalai Lama sat cross-legged, at his right a servant fanning him with a gold-handled yak-tail, while below him, along the face of the dais, was ranged a long row of yellow-capped priests, the sacred symbol of the Jewel in the Lotus embroidered on their claret-colored robes.

Side by side with the Tashi Lama, Jimmie pressed through the throng. Still the savage humming and chanting continued. It seemed like a great canticle of all Asia; terribly symbolic with a brooding, intense melancholia, without key, without distinct melody—just the rhythmic, staccato outpourings of Tibet's mysterious soul.

Then, suddenly, the chanting ceased. A trembling pause; a terrible void of silence; and, the next moment Jimmie heard a single voice speak out, high and sharp and clear.

He looked.

It was To Palté speaking, standing in front of the Dalai Lama.

"Hail—Jewel in the Lotus—hail!" cried To Palté. "We come to Thy feet today, O Living Buddha, to demand a sacrifice—the crimson sacrifice of war! This is the last day of the year—the lucky year—the year of the Wood-Dragon! The prophecies have spoken. The oracles have given word. They have told us to rise, to strike for Thy faith, for Thy salvation, O Jewel in the Lotus! The prophecies have ordered us to drive the foreigners into the sea!"

The monk turned, facing the assembly.

"Strike, brothers!" he cried. "It is war in the name of the Buddha! Whirl as the mill-stone whirls on its axis, relentless, resistless! Carry death into the ranks of the foreigners, and strike for the faith! Ah—the year of the Wood-Dragon!"

"The year of the Wood-Dragon!" came the wild echo.

By this time the Tashi Lama and Jimmie had pressed through to the front rank. The former touched To Palté on the shoulder.

"One moment!" he said. He drew himself up and addressed the crowd. "The final proph-

ecy has come! The final prophecy for which we
have been waiting! Tell us, Chandra Das!"

Jimmie bowed before the Dalai Lama who
looked down at him with kindly, weary eyes.

"Yes—" said the Dalai Lama, with a flat,
faint sigh, as if surrendering to the inevitable, to
fate. "Tell us, Chandra Das!" And, to the
multitude: "We shall abide by the final prophecy. Has not that been decreed by all the
oracles?"

"Yes, Jewel in the Lotus!" came the chorus.

Jimmie felt himself lifted up by a dozen hands,
found himself high on the shoulders of a gigantic
abbot. The mob had ceased to push and struggle. He saw below him a surging sea of faces,
staring up at him, expectant, savage, hysterical,
tortured into cruel grimaces.

For a second his nerve seemed to go. He felt
young and lonely, became conscious of a terrible
weakness in his knees, a sinking at the pit of his
stomach, and a catch in his throat. He remembered that he must hurry. For there had been
that delay in the Depon's message, and he must
tell it—with certain additions—before the Tashi
Lama received word from the border, so as to
make the prophecy plausible. And the Tashi
Lama was shrewd, even if he was superstitious.
He could not easily be fooled. On the other
hand the Tashi Lama did not know about the

peace party's quicker system of communicating through the hills, had no idea that word had reached Jimmie from the Depon through Ung Changren's lips.

A mixture of truth and gliding half-truths! A reliance on the Orient's blighting superstitions, yet without discounting the Tashi Lama's cleverness! That was the game which Jimmie would have to play—would have to play quick, since any moment the Tashi Lama's messengers might send word from the border; and he said to himself that he was one, against all these people, and alone, and young. Then again, suddenly, the thought came to him of the Chawkpore bazars. The friends of his boyhood days—Mehmet Tugluk Khan the Afghan and Gandra Rai the Hindu—if they could see him now! Wouldn't they envy him, though?

He pulled himself together with a great effort. The power of speech came back to him.

"The Buddha spoke to me in the night!" he shouted with his lusty young voice.

"What was the Buddha's message?" asked the Tashi Lama.

"The Buddha said that war would be a good thing—a just thing——"

"Hayah!" cut in the savage chorus. "War——"

"Yet—" went on Jimmie.

He could not make himself heard. His voice was drowned. But the Tashi Lama raised his hands, commanding silence with shrill accents and jerky gestures.

The crowd obeyed, waiting eagerly for Jimmie to speak.

"Yet war—said the Buddha—should not be made before the end of the year of the Wood-Dragon! On the other hand, if the Raj, before the end of the year should attack, then the Raj will be the victor—and, if that should happen, the Dalai Lama must sue for peace—said the Buddha!"

"Ho!" cried the Tashi Lama exultantly. "The end of the year of the Wood-Dragon! It is today! And the Raj—blind camel—has not attacked! It is war!"

He turned to the Dalai Lama.

"Give orders immediately, O Jewel in the Lotus! The prophecy is true!"

"No!" replied the Dalai Lama. "The end of the year is not yet!"

"What difference?"

"The Raj may yet attack! Messages have not yet come from the border! We shall wait——"

"But——"

"We shall wait!" repeated the Dalai Lama.

Then, as Jimmie was being lifted down from

the abbot's shoulder, as To Palté turned to the Dalai Lama, arguing that an hour made no difference, that, even if the Raj knew, it would be days before the sahebs would attack since they, like the fools they were, never made war before lengthy talks and discussions, while, on the other hand, every hour in hurrying mobilization meant a gain for Tibet, the Dalai Lama commanded him to be silent.

"We shall abide by the final prophecy, as we agreed!" he said. "The end of the year is not yet. Nor do we know what the Raj has done! If word comes before the end of the year that the Raj has attacked, we shall sue for peace—a white peace—a just peace—may the Buddha grant it!"

And when again To Palté argued, while the crowd hummed savagely, threateningly, the Dalai Lama rose. He was no longer the quiet, weary man.

"I am the Living Buddha!" he said in a voice as keen and dry as a new-ground sword. "My word is law. My gesture is a code. My whim is a decree. No decision shall be made about war until the end of the year of the Wood-Dragon. We shall wait—here—patiently——"

"But—" commented To Palté.

"Silence, dog!"

"Listen—listen——"

"Ah—" The Dalai Lama turned to the servant at his side with a quick, whispered word.

The servant jumped from the dais.

"Enforce my command!" cried the Dalai Lama.

And with utter, dramatic suddenness, the servant jerked a thick, short whip from his loose sleeve. He brought it down—once, twice, three times—across the monk's face.

"Akh!" cried To Palté, in an agony of pain. Blood spurted from his face. He fell, fainting, to the ground.

Silence, silence that floated like a balloon of evil anticipations.

"I am the ruler of this land," repeated the Dalai Lama, and there was in his voice an enormous, metallic resonance, the ring of utter conviction. "We shall wait—quietly—patiently!"

The reaction on the mob was instantaneous and typical. For these men were Asians, men in whom the cruelty and ruthlessness of a ruler excite admiration, as a conspicuous and unmistakable exhibition of energy. So silence fell over them like a pall. They waited, nervous, expectant, while the minutes dragged along on leaden feet—until, shortly before the noon hour, a travel-stained Tartar rushed into the "Outer Hall of the Gods."

"The messenger from the border!" came the hushed whisper.

"What is the news?" demanded the Tashi Lama.

The Tartar pressed through the crowd. He bowed before the dais.

"Hail—Jewel in the Lotus!" he said. "I bring news?"

"Tell us——"

"The Raj has attacked—suddenly—without declaring war! The Raj's guns are thundering at Rhari Fort! It is war—war——"

"No!" said the Dalai Lama. "It is peace! We shall abide by the prophecy!" He waved a hand. "The audience is over!"

He stepped down from the dais, addressed the Tashi Lama:

"Tomorrow you and I shall start for the border, together, there to conclude another treaty of peace and trade and amity with the Raj. A new treaty—a true treaty. The sahebs who are being kept prisoner shall accompany us——"

"And I?" asked Jimmie.

"You, too, Chandra Das!"

And it was thus that, the next morning, traveling in the Dalai Lama's caravan, Rankin and Jimmie, accompanied by the three C. A. C. C. agents, took the trail out of Lhassa to the border.

"Seems to me," said Rankin, "that these Tibetan monks offered you a whole lot of glittering rewards—if only you had teamed up with them and thrown that peachy little prophecy of yours their way! Well—we of the C. A. C. C. aren't exactly pikers, either! Jimmie—" he laughed— "name your own reward!"

"I want two!"

"Don't be so grasping! Well?"

"I want you to use your influence with the British-Indian government and have Ghula Khan released."

"No trouble about that, I guess. That Afghan roughneck is in ace high again with the British—he gave them a lot of information, you know. What's the second reward you want?"

"I don't want to be Jimmie any longer."

"Eh? Getting a swelled head?" smiled Rankin.

"No. But hereafter I want to be James Clinton Weatherby—of the C. A. C. C.!"

"Done! Three hundred rupees a month to begin with! Shake hands with your new boss, Mister James Clinton Weatherby—*alias* Jimmie!"

And they shook.

THE END